# Jesse

# 53$^{rd}$ Kentucky

## Ruth Ochs Webster

ISBN-13: 978-0-692-07463-3
ISBN-10: 0-692-07463-5

Ancestrals
An Imprint of
Tree Shadow Press

# Acknowledgements

Howard A. Young
Editor

Debra R. Sanchez
Tree Shadow Press

The Write Club
Critique Group

Hana Haatainen-Caye and members
Writers at Work

Stefanie Fontecha
Beetiful Book Covers

Philip R. Webster
Website Design

Barbara Matracia
Cook Family Photos

Cover Photo: Michael Turner © 123.RF.com

*Corporal Jesse J. Cook*
*is buried in Linden Grove Cemetery*
*Covington, Kentucky*
*With his comrades from the Civil War*

# Dedication

To all Sons of Kentucky

who bravely served their country

during our great Civil War.

United States or Confederate States,

blue or gray,

now resting side-by-side

in the Linden Grove.

You'll abide forever in

memory.

*By your patriotic devotion to your country
in the hour of danger and alarm—
your magnificent fighting, bravery, and
endurance—
you have maintained the
supremacy of the Union and the Constitution,
overthrown all armed opposition to the
enforcement of the laws,
and of the proclamation forever abolishing
slavery—
the cause and pretext of the rebellion—
and opened the way to the rightful
authorities to restore order
and inaugurate peace on a
permanent and enduring basis
on every foot of
American Soil.*

*General Orders No. 108
To: Soldiers of the Armies of the United States
From: General Ulysses S. Grant*

# Jesse

## 53rd Kentucky

# PART ONE

## SOMETHIN' BIG

*I was never sepia-toned. I came out of my ma squalling, with bright red skin and a shank of dark hair. I've been known ever since as having a bit of a temper, Scottish by descent, and English. All I know is my folks were some of the earliest settlers in the Ohio River Valley. Came on flat boats down the river from Pennsylvania and cross the mountains from Virginia. They fought in the Revolution and the War of 1812. I suppose I got their warrior spirit.*

*The image of me goin' into the army...I was 19 years old. Looked pretty good, didn't I, all prissy in my uniform? Handsome devil: dark hair, dark complexion, grey eyes. You couldn't move, you understand. You had to stand there as straight as one of the staves in a barrel before it's bent and worked into shape. You had to stand, and wait, and wait, until the man behind the camera box ignited his lamp and you were blinkin' stars.*

*A soldier's life is a bit like that. They make his image before anything happens...before his uniform is covered with muck, mud, vomit and blood...before it's torn, with buttons missin', and permanently stained...before the real waitin' begins—the waiting that tests a man to the bottom of his soul—the waiting that comes before he rides into Hell.*

# CHAPTER 1

**Crab Orchard, Kentucky**
**November 24, 1864**

"God, this is rank, Jesse." Peter Strong spat the chaw of tobacco as far from his horse as was humanly possible.

"Better'n chewin' on dust all day."

"You'd think being a Kentucky regiment in this here Union army we'd get better stuff. I'm questionin' if that was tobacco at all."

The long line of the 53rd Kentucky Mounted Regiment stretched as far down the pike as the two troopers could see. Another monotonous ride, broken only by the occasional farm or town where civilians might gather to watch them pass. But even that interest was waning by the third year of the war.

"Where ve goin' again, Jesse?" The voice was from the mount behind him.

"Krimmelbein, I told you already—Crab Orchard. It's a major station on the L&N Railroad."

"That's the Louisville and Nashville, in case you don't know that neither," laughed Pete. "Did they even have railroads back in Der Faterland?"

"Ah, let off him," said Jesse. He glanced at Pete, the buddy he had ridden with since the regiment was organized in their hometown of Covington in September. "Ought to be there soon, I think."

"I think they should have carried us by rail."

A cantering horse approached from the rear, its rider pulling alongside Jesse. "Corporal, town's about fifteen minutes down the road. We'll enter in formation. Keep your squad mounted until further orders."

"Sergeant."

"I still don't reckon why yer our corporal, Jesse," said Krimmelbein. "I'm older than du."

"My Uncle Frank's a private, Joe, and he's old, forty-four. In the 56th Ohio."

"You," snapped Peter, shifting in his saddle to glare at Krimmelbein. "You, not du. And it's not about age. It's about brains. Jesse's got brains. He's a bona fide tradesman, and a born leader. Aren't you, Corporal? You and your pa runnin' that cooper shop up in Covington. J.R. Cook's—isn't that the name of it?"

"Yeah, that's the name of it. Until I can rename it J.J. Cook's after me."

"Bully! Woo-hoo! Mister Cook's an enterprisin' young man."

"Shit," Jesse replied with a grin.

The line began to slow, Crab Orchard gradually coming into view. Twenty to thirty houses. A couple churches. The train depot. All nestled at the base of the Appalachian foothills. Jesse stood up in his stirrups to get a better look. An endless array of army tents flanked the town to the left. In the 53<sup>rd</sup>'s previous duty of protecting the railroad from Cincinnati to Lexington, they had never seen a camp that covered this much ground.

"We're gonna muster, Pete."

"Somethin' big at last, Jess. Big at last."

They put their horses to trot in step with the mounts preceding them. With colors aloft, amid the bugle's blare and the thundering of two thousand hooves, the 53<sup>rd</sup> entered camp.

****

"From what I've heard tell from the other boys, the 54<sup>th</sup> is here, the 39<sup>th</sup>, and 45<sup>th</sup>. The 55<sup>th</sup> is due in tomorrow—more Covington lads." Jesse continued to fry up salt pork and beans. His horse, and those of his five squad members, had long since been fed and groomed, the saddle and gear cleaned and stowed.

"The 55<sup>th</sup>," remarked Daniel West. "Weren't they the ones riding that train under attack last month? They were supposed to be guarding it, and we wound up rescuing them."

"Hell, yeah, that's them. They're greener than a blade of grass. Shoulda stayed in Covington, for all the good they'll do us, the lot of them," snarled Pete.

Jesse looked at the other men, quickly changing the subject. "There's still Rebs around these parts. Betcha that. All over Kentucky. Proof's in the rail lines always needin' repair. Maybe that's why they had us ride in."

Krimmelbein stretched out his large body, resting his back against a tree. "Jesse, where ve goin'?"

"I'm not privy to that, Joe. You know that. I did hear talk we was headin' south, towards Tennessee. We're gonna meet up with even more of our boys. All of us going to be under the command of General Stoneman."

"Stoneman!" barked Pete. "Ain't that the sumbitch who was called the worst officer in the army? The only high-and-mighty chicken gut stupid enough to get himself captured by the Rebs? We get him?" His outburst was met with a smattering of laughter.

"He's our son-of-a-bitch now, trooper. Mind your tongue." Sergeant Blackwood plopped down beside his men. Jesse caught a hint of amusement crossing his face. "Corporal, you got any coffee brewin'? And, Strong, stoke the fire. It's getting mighty chilly, and you need to be thinkin' on your place in this here army."

# PART TWO

## THE GOOD SON

# CHAPTER 2

## *Four Months Earlier*

**Louisville, Kentucky**
**Mid-Summer, 1864**

General Stephen Burbridge felt vindicated, pleased. *This should quiet my detractors,* he thought. The telegram that he was holding from Secretary of War Stanton gleamed golden:

*Your proceedings against disloyal persons in your command are approved. Your telegram has been forwarded to Major-General Heintzelman. The whole State of Kentucky is constituted a military district of the Department of the Ohio and placed under your command, with authority of a departmental commander . . . General Grant suggests that new organizations white and black shall be enlisted as infantry and mounted if you wish to use them as cavalry, which would avoid trouble in dismounting them when needed for infantry . . . Your mode of mounting cavalry by seizing horses of disloyal persons is approved, and you are authorized to seize all you can lay hands on; and if you do not need them yourself, turn them over to the Quartermaster's Department for general service.*

****

## Covington, Kentucky
## Mid-August, 1864

Riley Cook pulled back on the drawknife, notching the last of the staves needed to form the flour barrel upon which he was working. His oldest son, Jesse, was busily preparing the cresset, the iron basket which would be placed in the center of the barrel and lit, relaxing the wood fibers and making it easier for Riley to gradually hammer metal hoops tighter and tighter around the barrel. Both of them were perspiring in the August heat, even though they worked outside of the small frame cooperage that fronted on an alley a few blocks south of the Ohio River. "Would be more than pleasin' to get one of them gover'ment contracts for gunpowder," he said. "This war could do somethin' for us."

Jesse set down the cresset, stepping over to help his father arrange the staves vertically inside the metal hoop. "Do you believe what Uncle Henry told us this mornin'? That Peter Hamilton's been arrested for disloyalty? I like that boot maker."

Riley grimaced in disgust. "Of course, I believe it. The situation's gotten damn near impossible. How can a man prove his loyalty to the Union, 'cept by saying it?"

"Well, Hamilton must have said something against the army or government, or somethin' that angered somebody."

"I don't rightly know, Jess. I'm just glad that we got our permit from the Provost Marshall so we can stay in business. Too many are having to close their doors."

"Why d'ya think we did? Get the permit?"

"My suspicion, Son, is because of where we were born. All of us: your Uncle Henry, me, you, your brothers—all of us were born across the river in the North. We weren't born in Kentucky, so they don't see us as a threat. Don't see us as people who hanker for the slave-ownin' South or have relations hidin' in the hills."

"Permit or no, our business ain't too good."

"Ain't good at all." Riley stood up and stretched his back. "I think when we settled here we chose the wrong damn side of the river. Hell, just a couple weeks ago, one of them Union generals ordered pickets along the entire riverbank. Just in case we tried to ford it and do a little business in Cincinnati." He shook his head in disgust. "Cincinnati. Covington. The two cities are practically one and the same. Same people. Same river."

"We didn't know it would come to this, Pa."

"Not allowed to compete with the fellas on the northern bank . . . Absurd."

"I heard there's a new general taking command of Newport and Covington. Name's Burbridge. Wonder what he'll do?"

Riley looked at his handiwork, satisfied with the result. "Don't rightly know, Son. Just keep your mouth shut about all things political when outside this shop." He adjusted the last of the staves. "You hear me?"

Jesse gave his father a knowing nod, "If there's one thing you taught me, Pa, it's how to survive."

Riley met Jesse's gaze but made no attempt to reply. He looked at his handiwork. "This one's ready to fire. Light the cresset. We've got work to do."

# CHAPTER 3

**Late August, 1864**

Jesse strolled through the open doors of his uncle's broom manufactory, several blocks south of the Cook cooperage. The place was alive with the chatter of men closing up shop for the day.

Henry Cook was in the back alley, overseeing a final wagonload bound for the river docks. He gave a hearty slap to the drayman's shoulder before the fellow leaped aboard.

"Gotta love the Germans pourin' into this valley, Henry. Cleanest people this side of Heaven," said the man as he released the brake and began to nudge the horses from the alley to the street. "Doin' well for ya."

"This load's going to the army," replied Henry. "Hospitals, I reckon. Best customer there is, the government."

"GEE!" The team perked up slowly, beginning their pull.

Jesse strode up beside his uncle. "They told me you were out here."

"Jess! What brings you here, boy?" It was obvious from the grin crossing Henry's face and the arm that he threw around his nephew's shoulders that a deep affection existed between the two.

"Did Riley close early? Or did you high-tail it, leaving your pa fumin'?"

"I told him I wanted to stop by before you closed shop."

"You got somethin' on your mind. I can tell. Come on in. You can talk while I deal with these bills of lading."

Jesse followed the older man back into the manufactory. He sat down on a barrel, made by his father, no doubt. His uncle began to sort papers and run calculations on the high desk where he kept his business ledgers.

"Well? Spit it out. I can run production sums and listen to you at the same time."

"They're recruiting men for a new Kentucky mounted infantry regiment—right here in Covington. I read a notice tacked up at the newspaper. A Major Edwards is settin' up an office in the Engine House on Pike St. Five hundred dollar bounty for every man they accept."

His uncle whistled. "That's a particle of money, Jess."

"It takes a might of cooperin' to bring in that much profit."

"How long would you have to go for?"

"Only a year."

Henry paused, placed his boot on the lower cross board of the desk and looked hard at his nephew. "I take it you haven't talked this over with your pa, or ma."

"Nossir."

"I also take it you want to do this."

"Yessir."

"Jess, I've always cared for you like you was one of my own. You know that."

Jesse nodded.

"But, you need to talk through this with Riley. He's the one whose blessing you want, not me. I can tell you one thing. He ain't gonna like losing your labor, and your ma will hate the thought of you going off and being shot at."

"Pa's a first-rate cooper. He can produce. Theo's old enough to assist in some ways, and Pa could take on a man if need be."

"I hate to say it, Jesse, but you're overlookin' a couple things. There ain't no men to take on what with the war and government hiring. All Riley'd be able to find is some broken down war vet, or another boy. What were you planning on doing with the bounty?"

"Giving it to Pa, I guess. To help out."

Henry sighed. "You're too good a lad, Jess. Boneheaded sometimes. Your father will welcome that money—to be sure." He slouched back onto a high stool. "Your pa likes easy money. Always has. You know that."

Jesse swallowed the sourness in his throat as he rose from the barrel, slowly walking away from his uncle's stinging words—that his pa could consider him *easy money*. True enough words, but ones Jesse hated to hear.

"He was a convicted burglar in Illinois," Henry continued.

"He's good now. It's been three years."

"Is he, Jess? I hope so, for your sake, but I don't trust him. He's my brother. I care about him, but I don't trust him. Never have. Riley is always looking for the easy way. Ever since we were lads. He was always willing to take. Not much of a giver, I'm afraid."

"He was driven to it." Jesse had sworn to himself that he would not show weakness to the man whose character he admired above all others—only strength. And he really didn't like discussing his father. "He wouldn't hurt *me*."

"Probably not intentionally, but it's his nature, boy. He puts himself first. Some men are weak that way." Henry noticed the conflicted look on Jesse's face. He strode over to where his nephew was standing and grasped him by the shoulders. "I tell you what. Give half of the bounty to your ma and pa to help them over the rough spots. I know Riley's struggling . . . Then give the other half to me—for safekeeping. You're going to need that when you return."

"Wha'd'ya think for?" asked Jesse.

"For when you assume control of that foundering cooperage from your pa. Riley may be a fine cooper, but his business sense . . . I see a brighter future for you."

****

Jesse stayed out most of the evening. More and more he sought companionship outside the confines of his parents' home, his circle of relatives. He was restless, eager for something. *But what,* he thought. *War? Soldierin'? What I really need to do is get to Ripley and see Eliza. My sweetheart'll understand.*

The pert little ginger-haired miss was four years his younger, but that didn't matter. The girl was obviously ready to claim Jesse as her own. She was sweet and voluptuous—very womanly in her mid-teens. She hadn't been coy about granting him a kiss or two earlier in the summer, and gave every indication that more awaited.

Ripley, Ohio, a river town east of Cincinnati, was populated with Jesse's relatives. He had visited there periodically for as long as he could remember, and had known Eliza for most of that time.

On this hot, humid final day of August he wound up where he usually did on his aimless meanderings, at the river. Like many another boy who grew up along its shores, he felt its pull. He glanced upriver, against the current. *Pittsburgh,* he mused. *Heard that place is a bit like Cincinnati. And downriver lies the Mississippi.* Jesse looked in the opposite direction, watching the water coursing its way west. *Like to take a steamer that far. If I was a rich man. Have my own stateroom. 'Liza on my arm. Walkin' the deck. I'd like to see that Golderned big river. St. Louis. Memphis. New Orleans. Southern cities . . . Maybe after the rebellion is over.*

His thoughts were interrupted. A guy about his own age was staring at him. Jesse hadn't even noticed the fellow when he first plopped down on the riverbank. He was well-built, taller than Jesse, with a rakish grin and unkempt sandy brown hair that spilled over his forehead in the front and well onto his neck in the back. His clothes were common, a workman's clothes, but he certainly seemed sure of himself. He was leaning against the river-facing side of a storage shack. "You either just done sumthin you shouldn't've, or you're thinkin' of doin' sumthin I'd like to be a part of." He strolled over to Jesse and thrust out his hand. "The name's Peter Strong. Folks call me Pete."

"Jesse Cook."

"Glad to be of your acquaintance, Jesse Cook." Pete nodded towards the river and the now fading outline of the hills, buildings, and steeples of Cincinnati in the distance. "She's mighty pretty this time of day, with night comin' on. You can't see the filth."

"Yeah."

Without invitation or explanation, Pete sat down beside Jesse on the dry clay of the riverbank, shoving a stone into the water with his heel as he did so. "Can't recollect seein' you around these parts."

"Lived here nigh on three years now, since..."

"Since what?"

"Since my family moved here from Illinois."

"Illinois? Chicago? Golderned. I never lived anywhere but here."

"Not Chicago. Morgan County. By Springfield, where Abe Lincoln's from."

"Even better. So you was lookin' at the river thinkin' about goin' back?"

"Nope. No desire to go back there. I was just thinkin' on what's out there. You know, that I haven't seen. Haven't seen much." Jesse looked over at Strong. "Can't recollect seeing you around, either."

"Growed up here. I'm a laborer mostly. Been workin' on the bridge since spring. And you?"

"Cooper. My pa and I have a shop in the alley a few blocks south."

"Tradesman. Impressive. That sorta explains it."

"What?"

"Why you don't know one of the most famous gents in Covington, that's what. You've been cooped up in a cooper shop."

Jesse laughed at the fellow's impudence and attempt at humor. Then he pointed towards the huge stone bridge tower rising from the Covington shore, its sister tower now barely distinguishable on the far shore. "I'm amazed by this construction. You're kinda lucky to be a part . . ."

"Yeah, I suppose you would like buildin' things." Pete leaned back on the riverbank, the better to gaze upon the massive structure. "The guy that designed it is named Roebling. His son is the engineer in charge of building it. It's gonna be a suspended bridge, cables crossing the whole river. Imagine that. The main span 100 feet above the river."

"You seem to know a lot about it."

"I may be a laborer, but I'm not stupid." Peter hauled himself back to a seated position, squaring his shoulders in defiance. "I listen. I learn. Plan to do somethin' big myself one day."

"Hey, don't take offense."

"You wanna chaw?" Pete rummaged in his trousers pocket and held out a tobacco pouch to Jesse.

"Sure."

"It's the good stuff. Kentucky's finest."

"How'd you get Kentucky's finest?"

"Maybe you don't wanna know."

Jesse was warming quickly to this Strong fellow who was working to build the first bridge to connect Covington with Cincinnati, Kentucky to Ohio, the South to the North. "Do you know when she'll be finished?"

"Won't be me finishing 'er. I'm of age in a week. I'm goin' to squash the Rebellion."

Jesse felt a jolt of admiration. "You're joining up."

"As soon as I can. Mounted."

Jesse tilted his head and grinned. "The recruiter at the engine house. I read about it. That's my plan, too. I just have to . . ."

"Well, beat the Dutch, Jesse Cook. We could be comrades." He studied Jesse. "Yer not of age, are you?"

"I am so—nineteen. I'm old enough. I can do what I want. I just have to convince my pa it's the right thing to do."

"He doesn't want you to go?"

"He wants me in the shop . . . But the bounty might convince him."

Pete whistled, then said in a pirate's brogue. "He'd sell his own son for some pieces of eight."

"I can only hope."

With a laugh Pete urged, "Come on, Jesse. It's getting dark down here. Let's see what entertainment we can find before we both go off to fight for the Union."

****

The lagers Pete and Jesse had consumed only added to their new-found camaraderie. It was well past dark when the two of them decided that they should be going home. A night patrolman had suggested they be on their way when he encountered them outside the saloon, and their singing had been shushed in no uncertain terms by an irate hausfrau.

"This is a shortcut." Jesse dragged Pete around the corner of a slumbering residence, into an alley. "I know all the shortcuts."

They were literally stumbling in the dark.

Halfway through the alley Pete banged his shin on an upturned wheelbarrow and nearly tumbled to the ground. "Son of a bitch! We should have stayed on the street where there's a trace o' light."

"Shut it. You'll wake the dead," Jesse said quietly.

"Shortcut. Shortcut, he says. Next, I'll fall in a hole. You wanna git me killed 'fore I even enlist?"

Their eyes were slowly adjusting to the darker stretches of the alley. A slight gleam from a street lamp filtered in between buildings. A bit of moonlight. Pete had stopped, rolling up his trouser leg to determine if he was bleeding. Jesse said nothing, waiting for his chum to finish with his ministrations.

The sound of breaking glass startled them. Pete stood erect. Jesse held a finger to his lips, stock still against the fence behind him. Turning in the direction of the noise, they saw a couple of shadowy figures, but it was too distant to make out faces. It appeared that someone was entering a building through a broken window.

"Burglars?" whispered Pete. They were near enough that any loud sound might scare the miscreants away. "Let's get out of here. Get a patrolman." He took a couple steps back the way they had come. Jesse grabbed him.

"No time. They're thievin', and I know the folks who own that place. We can't just leave."

Pete swore under his breath but did not venture further. "What do you propose we do?"

"Watch . . . until they come out. Maybe somebody else heard it, too. Somebody else might come. We'll figure it out, but we can't just leave."

"Suppose we can always run like thunder if we have to," said Pete resignedly.

They moved forward in a crouch, along the fence, their gaze fixed on a brick building which loomed ever larger. Soon they stood, rigid with tension, at the corner of Mahoney's Grocery.

The wait seemed endless. *Maybe we shoulda just gone for help,* thought Jesse. *I've no weapon. Didn't bring my knife. No tools on me. What in tarnation am I thinking?*

"Those fellas are sloppy," breathed Pete. He gestured towards an object lying in the alley. *A chisel.* He bounded across the few yards to where it lay by the broken window, grabbed it, and hustled back. *Now we're ready,* he thought.

Sounds coming from the building caused them to hold their breath. Their view of the window itself was not head on, but they could see enough of the alley to figure out what was happening. A man came into view. They had heard him drop to the ground through the window opening. He was receiving pilfered goods, several bags tossed to him. Fortunately, he never glanced in their direction.

Another thud. A muffled exclamation, as a second burglar tripped and fell to the ground. He scrambled to his feet, limping. "Shit! I left the hammer in there and damned near kilt myself getting out."

"Shut your mouth. Leave it. Let's go." The two began running in the direction from which Jesse and Pete had come.

There was no time to think. Jesse reacted instinctively. With a voiceless rendering of the word *now,* and a nod to Pete, he tore out of the darkness and barreled into the burglar who was nearest him.

****

Jesse, grappling with his man, unexpectedly found himself on his hands and knees in a stranglehold. His vision began to blur as he struggled to loosen the pressure on his throat. *I can't bree. . .* Tears were filling his left eye—smashed by the burglar when he and Jesse had been flailing on the ground. He could taste blood oozing from his lips.

Shouting. Torch light. The pounding of boots. *Coming . . . Someone's . . . Coming.* His mind was screaming for relief. He felt his body weakening.

"Uu-uu-uh." An anguished grunt. The pressure slackened. Jesse felt the arm fall away from his neck, the weight on his back decrease. In a burst of energy, he threw the man off. The next thing he knew, Pete was helping him to his feet.

"Ya hurt?"

"I'll be okay. Thanks, Pete."

The torchbearers had arrived, lighting the scene.

"Which of you's the thiefs?" lisped a burly patrolman, his billy pointed menacingly at Pete. The patrolman was minus several teeth, a testament to past encounters.

"Not that boy." It was Mahoney, the storekeeper, who spoke. He stared at Jesse, then his eyed flitted to the broken window, to the goods from his store spilling out of the bags, to the prostrate bodies of the moaning thieves, and then back to Jesse. "Good God, boy. What are you doing here?"

"Taking a short cut," said Pete wryly. "Jesse knew a short cut home."

"That there's Jesse Cook, officer, the cooper Riley Cook's son. Shop's just up the way. T'other boy must be his friend."

"We spotted the burglars," continued Pete. "Did what we could to stop 'em. I wanted to run and fetch the law. Figured it weren't my fight." Pete nodded at the two patrolmen. "But Jesse here was determined to stay."

Mahoney was taking inventory of his purloined goods: kid gloves and hosiery, alpaca and velvet ribbon for trimming, fabric, pomades, bonnets, and six packages of pocket cutlery. A search of the thieves' clothing netted thirteen dollars in silver coin, and packages of razors.

Mahoney's wife, Rose, had come with the men. She and her husband had heard the intruders in the store, exited their upstairs living quarters by a side staircase, and ran in search of help.

Once the patrolmen and the few passersby had dragged off the burglars, Rose sought to care for Jesse. She and Mahoney insisted that Jesse and Pete come into the store, where Rose had bound Jesse's swollen eye with a poultice. "You poor dear. Does that feel any better?" The warm, liquid mass was soothing. She ministered to his split lip as well as the bruises on his neck.

Mahoney looked at Pete, who except for a torn shirt and a few nicks and bruises looked fairly fit. "Yer used to fightin'," he commented.

"Yeah. But I had a weapon." He showed the chisel to Mahoney. "They dropped this here in their hurry to get in yer store."

Mahoney shook his head. "Can't say I'd wanna get walloped with that. No wonder they was in the shape they was in."

"I used the butt end. Didn't wanna kill 'im. He was hurtin' already from fallin' out your window."

"Well, I thank ya, boy. You . . . and Jesse."

"Do you know who they were?" Jesse asked thickly. *God,* he thought. *My Pa . . . went to prison for the same fuckin' crime.*

Mahoney slumped down on to a nearby keg, the gravity of the night's events weighing him down. "Patrolman thinks they're Southern sympathizers. Maybe even that guerrilla Mose Webster's men. He's been terrorizin' the merchants all over the county. Mostly stores . . . but tell your pa and uncle to mind themselves. This town ain't safe."

"The patrolmen are cartin' them to army headquarters," offered Rose.

"Reckon once me and Jesse are in the new mounted regiment we'll put the kibosh on the likes of them," said Pete.

"You're going to the war?" cried Rose. "Oh! Your mother, Jesse."

# CHAPTER 4

## Early September, 1864

"Does this have anything to do with that row you were in?" Riley glared at his son. "I told you. I don't want you enlisting!" The fist that crashed down upon the pine table practically split its face.

Jesse glared back at him. "It wasn't a row." He was standing as far away from his father in the tiny kitchen as possible, clutching the cup of coffee that had been offered by his mother.

"I'm telling you, Son, you don't want to mess with people who go through windows in the night—you can get hurt."

"I guess you'd know about that." Jesse wanted to scream at his father. *It wasn't a row. We foiled a burglary, for God sake! Of our neighbors'. A burglary. Who foiled you back in Illinois?*

But that risky jab would go nowhere. Jesse pivoted back to his main point. Trying to hold his voice on an even keel, he urged, "You can't keep me from going. This regiment is what I want, and they're still recruiting. I'm of age. They'll take me, I have no doubt."

"War ain't no grand adventure, boy. You've seen the cripples. You've seen the orphans. The streets are full of . . ."

"Uncle Henry warned me you'd fight this."

"Henry. Blazes, boy! I'm your father! Not Henry . . . Yet, you go to him first."

Catherine Cook swept an anxious look from her husband to her son and back. She dared not look at Riley directly, meet his eye. He could be a violent man. She feared his anger, but he seldom took it out physically on her or the children. She did not want to look into Jesse's eyes either. She admired the man he was becoming, and prayed now that he could hold his own.

Riley shook his head and frowned. "You know, son, there's nothing glorious in killing." Catherine felt her body begin to tremble.

"It's my duty. It's every man's duty," Jesse stated.

"Duty? Fuck it. You don't see the sons of the high and mighty enlisting." Riley gestured in the general direction of the substantial homes erected by wealthy merchants. "They pay bounties to scum like us to do their fightin' for them."

"I'm not scum." Jesse set the coffee down. His blue-grey eyes bore into his father's for the first time. "If I don't join now, they'll call me eventually. There'll be draft after draft. There's no gettin' around it. I'm not married. I'm healthy. I can read and write and know a trade. This way, I can do my own choosin'. I can join a horse unit instead of being put in some infantry. I can get a bounty." He yanked his cap from his pocket and walked out the door.

Catherine began to weep softly. She turned back to the batter she was stirring, feeling the tension in her shoulders, worrying about the children who would be coming in to breakfast. The breakfast Jesse had not stayed to eat.

"Catty." Riley was behind her, his muscular arms coming around her. She wiped her eyes on the hem of her apron, turned slowly, and finally met his gaze. His handsome, rugged face was taut with pain. His eyes, unbelievably, were moist. "I don't want to lose him. Not. Jess. To a bloody deathtrap of a war. He doesn't have to go. Not yet. He might never have . . ." She could hardly hear his whispered words.

"Won't you talk to him, father to son?" pleaded Catherine. "You're not just his boss; you're his father."

"I'm not much for showin' feelings, Cat." Riley broke the embrace as quickly as he had formed it. "You tell him. He won't hear it from me anyway. His *Uncle Henry* has already approved of him going. I've done lost Jesse." Waving his cap, as if in surrender, Riley took one last look at his wife. "I'll be in the shop. If you would, send somethin' out with Theo for me to eat."

****

Jesse had not gone to the shop, nor the recruiting office at the Engine House. He walked off the anger towards his father. Up Scott Street. Down Madison. Over Fifth. Back over Fourth. Through the market place. Around the customs house. He thought about Peter Strong and considered his father's words. *Am I seeking a grand adventure because I liked the way it felt? The excitement? The violence? To be applauded for violence? Feel the hero? Is that what I'm doing?*

He had searched the area for Strong but saw no sign of him. *For all I know, he's joined up and gone.*

Jesse's mind jumped haphazardly from one bit of news to another as he made his way towards the river. It was over three years into the struggle, and the papers were full of fact, opinion, and rumor. Everything about the war fascinated him, and he was determined to be a part of it.

- By early September his home county of Kenton had over 8,500 men in the Union Army. Recruiting in the city had progressed briskly.
- The Attorney General of the United States had decided that colored soldiers would receive the same pay as white men.
- General Burbridge had ordered two cavalry regiments from Ohio and Michigan to Crab Orchard, Kentucky, but no purported Rebel invaders had been found. Still, the rumors persisted of an imminent invasion. A Rebel deserter reported that 30,000 Confederates were to be moved through Pennsylvania to Pittsburgh and then Cincinnati.
- The Democratic political ticket of McClellan and Pendleton was campaigning hard against Lincoln—determined to end the war and restore Constitutional government.

- In Covington, the military decided to no longer examine personal luggage and no permits were required for shipping family items.
- A private from the 59<sup>th</sup> Ohio Volunteers, arrested for stealing a watch, told the judge that he would rather go to jail than back into battle.
- Draft resistance movements were growing throughout Ohio, Indiana, and Illinois.

Jesse stopped short when he came in view of the ferryboats docked at the Covington shore. Shuffling lines of dirty, haggard men were being herded onto vessels under the supervision of armed Union soldiers. They appeared to have come from the direction of the train depot.

A grizzled coachman had pulled his horse to a halt not far from where Jesse stood. "Heard they're Reb prisoners. Captured—Battle o' Atlanta."

Jesse nodded.

The man continued. "Pro'ly on their way to Camp Chase in Columbus." He stared at Jesse. "How cum yer not off to war? Look fit to me."

"I'm more than fit," replied Jesse, "And I will be gone. Matter of days. One of the new mounted regiments."

"Good for you, lad." The man pointed towards the hapless prisoners. "Just don't wind up like them—or worse."

\*\*\*\*

Jesse found his mother alone in the front room of the small frame house which abutted the cooper shop. She was busily altering a pair of Jesse's outgrown trousers to fit his younger brother. The room was stifling. Nary a breeze carried through the lone open window. Perspiration glistened on her face and forearms. Strands of hair hung limply from her failing bun, so fresh when she had pinned it up that morning.

"Why don't you do that outside?" he asked, catching her eye as she looked up.

"Where have you been, Son? Your pa is grousing you haven't been to help him all day."

"Walkin'. Thinkin'."

"And?"

"I didn't get enlistment papers yet, if that's what you wanna know."

Catherine scooped up her sewing and stood. "It is ungodly hot in here. Come out with me. I'd like to talk to you."

Jesse hauled out a pair of stools, positioning them in the only shade he could find in the strip of dirt and scrub grass that constituted their side yard. They had no proper porch.

Before his mother could say a word, Jesse pulled out part of a folded newspaper that was stuffed in his vest pocket. He proceeded to unfold it, careful not to rip the newsprint. "Listen to this." He began to read. "President Lincoln has ordered that on Wednesday, the 7th day of September, commencing at the hour of 12 noon, there shall be fired a salute of 100 guns at the arsenal at

Washington, and at New York, Boston, Philadelphia, Baltimore, Pittsburgh, Newport, KY, Saint Louis, New Orleans, Mobile, Pensacola, Hilton Head, New Berne, or the day after the receipt of this order, for the brilliant achievement of the army under command of Major-General Sherman in the State of Georgia, and the capture of Atlanta." He paused, almost breathless. "Ma, we'll hear the guns from Newport right here, sure enough. But I still might yen to cross the Licking and hear them up close."

"I can't imagine Atlanta, exactly. What it's like, but it's a big place. It must be as big as Cincinnati." Catherine sighed. "Atlanta. Captured. All those people. Women. Children. Babies. My God."

"And if Atlanta's fallen, Ma. This war has to be almost over. Don't you think?"

"What are you trying to say, Jesse?"

He bounced forward on the stool, refolding the paper in a fan shape as he did so. "I don't want to miss everything, Ma. I should be doing my part. It's important. Heck, I prob'ly won't even fire a gun. No Rebs left. No need."

Catherine reached out and touched her son fondly on the cheek. "Jesse, like it or not, you are so much like your father. You want the adventure. Call it duty if you will, but you want the adventure. All men do." Her hand dropped back into her lap. She slumped on the stool, her back resting against the rough planks of the house. She looked past Jesse now, into memory. "And like your father, you tend to talk around things. Pull the wool o'er the eyes of the l'il pioneer girl who can't read nor write . . . I was born there, you know. In those Virginia hills. Some of those fellas you call Rebs are prob'ly cousins of mine. Cousins of yours, Jess. And they'll be lying in wait for you. Not all defeated. Not admittin' to it anyways."

"You're no better than Pa. I thought you'd understand," complained Jesse.

"Did you hear me say I don't approve? I said no such thing. I know you'll be goin', that there's no keepin' ya here. It's just that you could be fighting our own."

Jesse stood, as if he were about to leave again. "Not likely, Ma."

"It's just . . . It's just that we love you, Jesse. Me and your Pa. I almost can't bear the thought . . ." She rose in an attempt to embrace him, the sewing sliding from her lap into a heap on the ground.

"Nothing is gonna happen to me, Ma. It won't be like Cousin John Ramsey, or Eliza's Uncle Samuel." Jesse bent over to retrieve her work. "I don't expect no battles like Shiloh or Stones River, and I'll come back to Covington and run this ole cooperage when the war's over." He leaned over to graze her cheek with a kiss. There was no mistaking the taste of her tears. "Don't worry so much, Ma. I'm gonna be a good soldier. You'll see."

"When your cousin, John, was killed. We were all so a'grieved, and now . . ." Catherine rummaged in her apron pocket. "This came today." It was a letter. "Your Pa already read it to me. His brother Frank Cook is enlistin'. Scared of being drafted."

"Uncle Frank? What?"

"Yes. Ohio Volunteers. I'm sure it's the bounty. Him, older than your father even, with younguns' still at home. I feel like this war is gonna tear our family apart piece by piece." She straightened her back, regaining her composure, to look up intently at her firstborn son. "It's a horse regiment you'll be joinin', then?"

He put both of his hands on her shoulders; his excitement evident. "Yeah. Imagine it, Ma, me up on a fine horse. Jesse Cook, trooper, in the United States Army."

"I know how you take to animals. You'll like that."

"You've seen the cavalry, Ma. You've seen them ride through town. Five hundred horsemen. Glorious."

"Yes, Jess, you'll look fine sittin' that horse. All your brothers'll be wantin' to ride with ya." She managed to stifle the cry forming in her heart. "Now, please go to the shop and help Riley for a while. And, Jess, tell him I told you."

"Told me what?"

"He'll know."

As he bounded away from her, his step more lively than she'd seen in days, one thought crossed her mind. *Not knowing will be the worst.*

****

Riley tipped the completed keg onto its side, setting it in motion with a swift kick of his heel. It began to roll towards the others, already stacked and ready for delivery. The day's work was playing hard on Riley's body. His shoulders ached. His back ached. *How does a man do this when he's fifty?* he thought. *Much less sixty . . . If'n I don't have my sons.*

Jesse appeared at the shop entrance, stopped, and gazed silently at his father. He stood there with all the self-assurance of the young, the confidence that Riley could no longer taste, a contagious restless spirit. He was nonchalantly chewing on a sweet honeysuckle vine, no doubt ripped from the strand on a neighboring fence.

"So you decided to do some work," commented Riley mildly. "Bit late in the day."

"I just finished talking with Ma."

"And?"

"I think she wants you to say I can go with your blessing."

"Did she tell you her concerns?"

"She told me. I tried to make her understand. It won't be that dangerous, Pa. They said we'll be protectin' the railroad and such . . . Even Uncle Frank has enlisted."

"Yes, I know." Riley shook his head in disbelief. He wiped his hands and brow on his shirttail, plopping down on one of the kegs, allowing himself a respite. He felt ancient, at all of forty-two. "How do you know when a boy becomes a man, Jess?"

His son seemed baffled. "Eighteen? That's what the government decided."

"The government had to set some age," replied Riley, "but that's what they call arbitrary."

"Nickel word," smiled Jesse.

"The truth is, it depends—on the man, on the boy."

"So, what do you think, Pa? Am I a man or a boy?" Jesse could feel his face begin to flush. He did not want to show any emotion, have his father belittle him.

Riley shook his head, bemused. "A year ago, a few months ago, if you'd have asked me . . . But, look at you now. You're taller than me. You're stronger than me." Jesse began to feel uncomfortable under his father's inspection. "But that's not what I'm gettin' at. You become a man when you can decide for yourself. When you can decide, and you know why you're decidin'. Right or wrong."

"Do you think I'm right or wrong to wanna go?"

"It don't matter what I think, Jess. You're a man now. Hell, you've been mostly a man ever since you was fifteen, when I . . . ."

"Went to prison?" Jesse finished his father's sentence.

Riley nodded towards the stack of kegs, but could not answer his son directly. "Would you give me a hand, loadin' those in the wagon?"

"Sure, but what's your decision about me joining up? What's this talk of being a man or not a man. Do I have your support?"

Riley gave his son a sad smile. "What you decide, I will live with. I've no doubt that you know exactly what yer doin'."

He glanced at the kegs. "Give me a hand with these now. We've got to load that wagon, so I can deliver them at sun up."

"I'll be glad to rise early and take care of it, Pa." Jesse strode over to the waiting kegs, hoisting the first of them and placing it in the wagon. "Our old nag likes me better than you." He laughed. "Besides, I need practice. I have a notion I'll be risin' early in the army."

"I expect you're right about that, Son. I also know that whatever regiment you're signin' up for is damned lucky to be getting you."

# CHAPTER 5

**Ripley, Ohio**
**Late September, 1864**

They cut romantic figures on horseback. They always did—young mounted troopers. These three were no exception, despite the dust on their boots, the rumpled appearance of once-pressed dark blue jackets, and the unshaven whiskers of days on the road. They had paused at the top of the embankment that would lead down to the river ferry in Augusta, on the Kentucky side of the Ohio.

Jesse rode in the center of the three, proudly sporting the double chevron of his newly-granted corporal's rank. His sabre was clearly visible: attached near the saddle horn, brass hilt shimmering in the noon-day sun, the scabbard resting between his left leg and the horse. Carbines were holstered near the men's right legs; pistols readied at their belts.

Private Peter Strong rode on Jesse's right. On his left was Private Daniel West, both members of the corporal's newly formed platoon in Company B of the 53rd Kentucky.

"Soon," Jesse said, "Eliza." To which remark Pete only smiled and shook his head. The troopers urged their horses forward at a walk, needing to queue behind two farm wagons, a cart, a beautifully appointed barouche, and a couple of civilians on horseback. All to be summarily searched by the military guard: vehicles, loads, and passengers.

After years of enduring security measures on the Covington to Cincinnati crossing, Jesse was accustomed to the process. This would be his first crossing, however, as a soldier on a military pass. A soldier in the Union Army. A ferryman waved to Jesse, signaling that the troopers should come around to the front of the line.

"You two stay put until I see what's going on." Jesse set his mount, Pretty, on a slow trot, so as not to disturb the other animals or passengers in front of him.

"Corporal, state your business."

Jesse removed orders from his jacket pocket and handed them down to the guard, noting that the soldier was a member of a local militia unit. "Permission to cross. Orders of Cap'n Haggarty. 53rd Kentucky. Final visitation before headin' south."

The soldier made a cursory examination of the document before handing it back to Jesse. "'Peers in order. Go ahead and board. Walk yer horses."

"Much obliged." Jesse turned in his saddle, motioning for Pete and Danny to ride forward. He patted Pretty lovingly on her bronzed neck, hoisted his body, and slid effortlessly to the ground.

****

The ferry berthed with a slight bump on the Ohio side of the river. Lines were tossed and secured, the plank lowered, and soon the troopers led their horses ashore, taking them first to the water's edge for a much-needed drink.

"Let's drive," said Jesse as he impatiently remounted Pretty, urging her up the bank to the River Road. "Ripley awaits."

He did not know if Eliza would be aware he was coming. He had written, but postal delivery to the small river towns like Ripley was often sporadic. They had already visited relations of Danny's. Jesse thought of the grandmother, whom they had just left that morning. *I expect that dear woman is still recuperatin' from seeing Danny in uniform. She about swooned. Hope Eliza doesn't do that . . . Liza would never do that. Too willful.*

He glanced over at Pete, who was mostly along for the ride. For safety's sake, the army wanted more than two on the road.

"Eleven miles," Jesse commented. "We should be there in a couple hours, well before dinner." *And there's others to visit. Gotta go to the farm tonight. They'll bed us. There's others I gotta see in town. But, Eliza first. Liza. First.*

****

Eliza Jane Fennell tugged the last of her unmentionables off the clothesline, heaving them into the basket. They had dried quickly in the soft autumn breeze. At fifteen, she had fully grown into her womanly endowments and reveled in the persuasion she seemed to wield over men. She felt their responses when she hoisted her skirt to show a bit of ankle or leg as she climbed steps or avoided puddles or mud. She felt the effect her ample bosom produced when obediently following the advice to "stand up straight, dearie." It didn't seem to matter if she was plainly clothed. She felt men's admiration.

The old men and boys of Ripley meant nothing to Eliza, however. She was in love with Jesse, her dashing young soldier. Taking his letter from her apron, she leaned against her parents' house, imagining his dark hair flopping over those sleepy blue eyes. She felt her fingers tracing the outlines of his face, gently pushing aside the pesky strands. Allowing her tongue to gently moisten her lips, she remembered his kisses. *What will he look like in his uniform?*

She was clutching the letter to her breast, her eyes momentarily closed, when she heard the sound of hoofbeats . . .


## Two Days Later


Jesse, Pete, and Danny had come for dinner at the Fennell household. Somehow, Eliza's ma, Martha, had stretched the meager fare to feed three additional mouths, for which Jesse was most appreciative. John Fennell was merely a laborer, working where he could, when he could. Some of what lay on the table appeared to be offerings from the recent harvest, largesse perhaps of an employer, perhaps from Jesse's own Gentry relations at whose farm the young men had spent the night. But their farm was hardscrabble, so he doubted that.

"We'll be leavin' at first light tomorrow," said Jesse. "Have to catch the early ferry crossing. Meet up with our regiment. It'll involve some hard ridin'."

"Personally, I'd linger on here," said Pete. "You're most hospitable folks." He smiled at Eliza. "But the corporal here will not allow me to malinger."

"'At's right," remarked John Fennell. "You boys have a duty to fulfill. Jesse for one'll see to that. I knowed him since he was a wee lad."

"Did you folks hear the news comin' out of Cincinnati about the deserters?" Jesse asked. "The Gentrys told us about it. Then I read me the newspaper account."

"Heard some such, but don't know all the details."

"A large proportion of the 450-some persons drafted last week have deserted. A large portion." Jesse continued animatedly. "The provost marshall told the *Times* that when the government desires volunteers they expect to get the double-extra article, and are willing to pay a handsome sum for it."

"You boys are that. The guvmint couldn't do better'n you."

"You're worth every cent of those bounties," commented Martha.

"And," Jesse said. "When they draft, an inferior article will sometimes answer. A man who would not be worth a big bounty as a volunteer, will do as a conscript."

"And then they just up and disappear," said Danny.

"How are your Ma and Pa takin' to you soldierin', Jesse?" asked Martha.

"Neither of them liked it in the beginning. Ma just worries too much, and, frankly, Ma'm, Pa did not want to lose my labor in the shop." He gave her a sheepish grin. "You both know my pa. The bounty helped ease the pain of my leavin'."

****

Pete swung up into the saddle. The autumn air had chilled considerably since the sun set. "Don't worry about it, Jesse. You stay here and say a proper good-bye to Liza. If you're waylaid on the road by some Rebel spy, I will take full responsibility for your demise." He yanked his horse's reins and fairly bolted from the Fennell homestead.

"See you back at the farm, Corporal," said Danny, setting out after Pete.

Jesse heard Eliza softly approaching him in the darkness. He had not heard a door open or close, thought she had stayed inside when they had made their good-byes to the family.

"You did not leave with them," she said. "Ma and Pa will think you've all gone."

Jesse was holding Pretty's reins. Motioning for Eliza to follow, he began leading the horse quietly away from the front of the house, around the corner and down an alley. As far as they could get from prying eyes.

"What's this place?" Jesse whispered.

"Old man Talbot's stable. He's gone."

"To the war?"

"Dead."

"Oh . . . then it's empty."

"Far as I know, Jesse."

He pulled Pretty into the unoccupied structure and wrapped her lead around a post. Before turning to Eliza, he removed the belt and holster from his waist, carefully draping it over the saddle.

In the dark, he could scarcely make out Eliza's features. Soon enough, though, his left hand settled on the ginger curls protruding beneath her bonnet. With his right, he loosened the ribbon tie. Eliza obliged him, removing the bonnet herself and allowing it to fall to the ground. Unbound, her hair tumbled in a thick mass around her face and neckline.

Jesse thrust both of his hands into the mass of curls, pulling Eliza to meet his kiss. She moaned. He deepened their kiss, allowing his tongue to dance across her lips, knowing she would respond in kind. His tongue met hers.

Locked in embrace, they gradually sank to the soft earth of the stable floor, covered as it was with straw and wood chips—first kneeling, then collapsing in a heap of gasping breaths and murmured affections. Jesse's fingers tentatively brushed her breast. When she did not flinch, his hand closed in a caress. Her hands cradled his head, stroked his face, kneaded his shoulders and arms. They were kissing: lips, cheeks, nose, the nape of her neck, the side of his.

So closely entwined. All arms and legs and clothing. Rolling over. Still kissing, growing ever more heated.

Jesse groaned, his feelings moving beyond his control. "Liza . . ."

"Jesse."

"I should go."

"Don't leave me." Her hand brushed below his waist. "Jesse . . ."

He moaned.

She grasped his hand, his arms, pulling him above her. Tugging at her skirts, yanking them above her waist. Inviting. Ready.

"Liza, we shouldn't . . . Should?" He could scarcely breathe. The skin of her bare legs, her belly, felt like fire smoldering through him.

"Yes, Jesse. Now." She helped him free himself, feeling a woman's power surge through her. *Jesse. Nothing else matters,* she thought. *Jesse.* She confidently opened to him, in her ardor pushing aside the remnants of straw, the wood chips. *Jesse.* Suppressing the desire to cry out . . .

*Oh, Jesse.* She bit her lip, overriding the pain, the fear, the uncertainty. "Jesse," she cried aloud.

"Oh, God." *Leaving . . . might never return . . . My soldier.* She dug her fingers into Jesse's back, and tore at his hair.

****

Tears coursed down Eliza's cheeks. Jesse knew she had been crying. They had simply lain in each other's arms. Spent. Quiet. Now, wanting to comfort her, he dried the tears with his fingertips and kissed where they had run. Struggling to his knees, he lovingly helped Eliza do the same, pulling her into a position where they could meet face to face in the darkness. Taste each other's breathing. He straightened her skirt, covering her, and held her close to share his warmth. They were both trembling.

"Eliza," he stammered. "Eliza, sweetheart." He paused, not being sure of the words. "When I . . . When I . . . Wait for me, Liza. Will you . . . wait?"

"Wait to marry? Yes . . . Only you."

Pretty snorted, then gave Jesse a shove with her lowered head. "What the thunder?" he exclaimed, taken by surprise.

Eliza laughed, reaching up to stroke the horse's nose. "If it's agreeable with your horse, I will wait. I think she wants to be your sweetheart, too, Corporal Cook."

Eliza allowed herself to sink deeper into Jesse's embrace as he maneuvered the two of them out of the animal's reach.

# CHAPTER 6

**Cynthiana, Kentucky**
**Mid-October, 1864**

The non-commissioned officers of Company B listened attentively to the briefing being put forward by Captain Haggerty. Jesse and Stuart Perry, a fellow corporal, leaned against a parked wagon. Their first camp was still in the early stages of being constructed, well in sight of the train depot. They would headquarter in an existing brick building commandeered by the army, but an adequate stable area and other out-structures needed to be constructed. Gear and material littered the landscape. The congenial but purposeful conversation of men at work blended with the sounds of saw, hammer, and ax. And, in the background, the ever-present smell, snorting, shuffling, and occasional neighing of over a hundred tethered horses.

"We are here for a definite reason, one reason only, to protect the railroads—line and stock. This town, Cynthiana, has been firmly in Union hands since the defeat of John Hunt Morgan in June; and, with his demise in Tennessee, we do not anticipate a reprisal of those engagements." The captain cleared his throat, adjusted his spectacles and commenced reading from a folded newspaper. "Three days ago, in the morning, about six o'clock, a gang of twenty-five Rebels under the command of Pete Everett, tore up the track of the Kentucky Central Railroad one mile south of Lowe's Station, which is about midway between Paris and Lexington. The morning passenger train from Covington came along in a few minutes afterward, and was immediately attacked by the Rebels, who fired into the cars, killing a negro and wounding three white men and one negro. The engine and tender ran off the track, and the cars destroyed by fire. Nearly all passengers were robbed. Everett took $2,700 from the Adams Express Company, and $40 and a watch from the conductor . . . The passengers were sent on to Lexington . . . Everett and men left for parts unknown. The passenger train returned to Covington."

"This activity is too close to home for my comfort," Jesse hissed to Stu.

"And mine."

The captain continued. "On the previous evening, guerrillas plundered Carrollton, leaving with about $1,500 in goods. Men, I need not remind you that Carrollton sits directly on the Ohio River, a stone's throw from home. The danger is real and present." He paused, allowing the men to consider the import of what he was telling them. "Passenger trains pass daily through Cynthiana from Covington and points north. This is a strategic point on the road. Very important to the Union cause that it remain open and unimpeded."

The captain folded the newspaper a bit tighter, inserting it into his coat pocket. He then looked out over the men, scanning their faces, eye to eye.

"The lieutenant, here, will continue this briefing, informing you of our plans to deploy your squads—where and when. Before I leave, though, I want to address a rumor that is circulating and assure you that the Army has matters well in hand. The Rebels who attacked the railroad proclaimed that they were an advance guard connected to a mounted force of considerable numbers descending upon us. All under the command of Breckinridge. This story is not probable, but General Burbridge has ordered General Hobson to send scouting parties from Mt. Sterling to Prestonburg, and on all other roads by which a force might move into Kentucky, either by the Pound Gap or Louisa Fork road. They will retard the advance of any force they may find, by skirmishing, felling trees, et cetera."

Captain Haggerty nodded at the enlisted leadership of his company, his way of offering full support. He then donned his hat, reciprocated the salute of the lieutenant, and strode off in the direction of the construction.

****

Jesse and Stu spent the remainder of the day supervising their squads in fatigue duty, which on this day amounted to leveling out rudimentary roads in the new stabling area.

Pete tamped down more dirt with a shovel; his boots, trousers, shirt, face, and hands every bit as brown as the earth. "Will this be my weapon of choice?" he groused. "I'm more familiar with the feel of this shovel handle than my rifle stock."

"Oh, stop complaining, Pete. It's lookin' good," said Jesse, who was attacking some lumps of dirt on his own. "Your next line of work could be road-building. I'll recommend you."

"Very funny." Still, Pete had to smile. This was such a far cry from what the two of them had envisioned when they discussed soldiering. "And, you, Corporal, are definitely destined to be the boss of that cooperage. You were born to it."

"Which makes me wonder," said Danny, "why someone as experienced as you, Corporal, working with wood your entire life, is not over there with the carpentry fellas."

"Which would have all of us over there with the carpentry fellas," replied Pete. "I was workin' on the bridge, Danny, remember? THE bridge that's crossing the Ohio. Should I be digging a road? I ask you to consider that."

"And I would have you consider," said Jesse, "that we left our civilian selves back in Covington."

Pete was about to offer a rejoinder, except for the approach of Stu Perry and the other members of their platoon, shovels shouldered, making their way towards them.

"We're done in, Jesse," announced Stu. "It's mess time. Startin' to get dark."

"I'm with you, Stu. My boys have moved enough dirt for one day. It's making them downright ornery. Let's pack it in, bubs, and follow Corporal Perry."

"Isn't this why God invented mules?" groused Pete as he stretched his aching back. "And oxen. Even dogs. To do our work? I did not enlist for this."

"Uncle Sam shoulda conscripted a mule and left you back in Covington," laughed Joe. "It would be more pleasant. Vee Germans, vee know how to work."

"Krimmelbein, when you learn to speak like an American, I'll respect your opinions."

"I am American," Joe bristled.

"Pete. Joe," barked Jesse, thrusting his shovel in their direction. "You two need to get along. You make me feel like your Golderned papa. Now, let's go."

"Ah, Corporal." Joe looked contrite as he began to shuffle in the direction of their quarters. Pete merely grinned.

"We're all on the same side," Jesse reminded them.

****

*This is the duty that suits me,* Jesse thought. *Sure, I'll be that living example that every corporal is meant to be: the first to fall into ranks, tent and bunk always in order, capable of instructing recruits in tactics. But this—Corporal of the Guard—this is real soldiering.*

He and Stu were on their rounds, ready to relieve the sentinels from a two-hour shift. They had long since completed another of their duties, supervising the nightly meal with the mess.

There were three guard stations posted around the perimeter of the camp. It was a small detail, reflecting relative safety. After having met with the sergeant of the guard earlier in the day, Jesse and Stu had posted a list of soldiers who would man the reliefs under their watch. The replacements now fell in behind Jesse when he approached. Stu, being the corporal of the old guard, accompanied him.

"Support—Arms! For'ard! March!" commanded Jesse.

The small band set off in the direction of the post where the first soldier was stationed. When the sentinel sensed relief approaching, he stopped marching and faced them, his rifle at the shoulder.

"Relief! Halt!" Jesse had stopped his men about six paces from the sentinel. He then commanded. "Number one! Arms! Port!"

The sentinels, old and new, with their rifles at ready, approached each other. At Jesse's direction, the soldier being relieved whispered the instructions to the new man. This done, both shouldered their arms. The former sentinel passed in quick time, taking his place in the rear of the relief behind Stu.

Once more Jesse commanded, "Support—Arms! Forward! March!" He had two more men to relieve as quickly as possible. *And then I need to get back here and visit each one of them to make sure that they know their duties and perform well. I'll be the one held responsible. No missteps tonight.*

# CHAPTER 7

## Cynthiana, KY
## The Mail Wagon

*Camp in Cynthiana Oct 15th 1864*

*Dear Ma and Pa*
*I will answer everything I can from two letters I have received from you. All the rumors of invasion are just that, rumors. None of that is true. We hear it too. It is quiet here. Nothing is happening. We eat sleep drill and go on patrol, and that is all . . . I have never taken my pistol out of the holster . . . You would like my new coms. They are hearty fellows. When we are not too tired we play draughts, cards, and baseball. I am not good at that game. I hit the ball right into a barrel of our drinking water. I don't know who the cooper was, Pa. Not as good as me or you . . . There is a chaplain here who preaches twice every Sunday when the weather will admit. We also have prayer meeting every night. I go when I don't have guard duty . . .*
*Your son*
*JJ Cook*

\*\*\*\*

Camp in Cynthiana Oct 19$^{th}$ 1864
Dear Uncle Henry
I have fired my gun. My boys and I and our sergeant sometimes go out on patrol every day. Oftentimes we are behind the guerrillas. We see what they have done. We don't see them. We try to clean up what ever damage they have done but mostly we call in work crews . . . I did shoot my rifle. We saw or more like heard men scampering into the woods. Shadow soldiers I call them. We fired into the woods and I think we shot one of them. Heard a yowling. We were not going to ride into the woods and get ambushed. We waited a while and then went in. Found no body, not even the wounded fellow . . . One day we discovered a cart full of stones left on the tracks of the Ky Central RR On a bridge. It probly would have derailed a passenger train. Maybe not a big freight locomotive. We removed the cart . . .
Your nephew
JJ Cook

\*\*\*\*

Covington, Ky.
October 25, 1864

Dear Jesse,
All the news here is about the election. The Democrats are determined to unseat Lincoln. They caution that Gen. McClellan is the last hope for an

*honorable peace. John Scott Harrison, son of William Henry, spoke at Greenwood Hall in favor of McClell. At Mozart Hall the Peace Democrats denounced McClell. and sought to pick a different candidate. It's bull, Jess—every word from the Democrats mouths. Any man in the county who was a Confederate soldier or served in any way with that govt is not allowed to vote. All saloons in Covington and Newport are ordered closed on the night of the election. Any violation will be met with the confiscation of liquor by the military police . . . It is believed that 70% of soldiers will vote for Lincoln. I assume you are a Lincoln Man . . . Not every soldier is confident in the outcome of this war. A fellow in the 183rd OVI despaired, killed himself by jumping off a boat docked at the foot of Main St. . . . I have every faith in you, son.*

*Yours,*
*Uncle Henry S.*

****

*Covington Oct 27th 1864*

*Dear Son*
*It is impossible to conduct business in these times. Do not concern yourself. The cooperage is the same Orders about the same as previous to when you departed. Theo has stepped up and is doing a fair enough job for a scrawny lad of thirteen . . . It's the*

*hog trade that makes me shake my head. You will shake yours too at this idiocy. First a general sends out a call for hogs from Kentucky promising a fair market value. The colonel in command of Covington and Newport then stops the shipment of hogs from Kentucky to Ohio. Why? Fear of southern hogs? And Where are the slaughter houses? Cincinnati. Always bet on the high card, Jess. The general won the hand . . . Within weeks the good colonel reverses his decision saying that the restrictions on hog trading do not apply to the loyal citizens of Kenton Campbell and Bracken counties. All they need are special permits from the Brd of Trade. I read in the paper today that 1100 hogs out o' Maysville crossed the river yesterday. Who knows what will happen Tomorrow? How will we get on without the army when this is over?*

*I know youll be interested in the draft news. Senator Wade wanted to postpone the supplementary draft in Hamilton County but the provost marshal told him to proceed. The prov. marshal also made an address about the draft at the Campbell County Court House. There's an ongoing rivalry between Kenton and Boone counties on filling our draft quotas. "The Commercial" reported that agents from Boone County are recruiting Kenton County men which deprives us of our own men . . . I wonder what in blazes they are offering. . . I wrote down these numbers to tell you. Kentucky has 955 draftees 15,300 volunteers and 3,057 veterans now serving. Keep your spirits up, son. Let me know if you need anything. Supplies. Or anything we can send you.*

*Your time will soon pass and I am in hopes that peace will come and you will get home before your year is up.*

*Your father*
*Jos. R Cook*

\*\*\*\*

*Camp in Cynthiana Oct. 27<sup>th</sup> 1864*

*Dearest Eliza*
*I do think that you are foolish to cry so much, for it don't do you or anyone else any good. You may injure your health . . . If it was not for you I wouldn't be writing by my candle tonight. The thought of your sweet smile is all the company I have. Your sparkling blue eyes and rosey red cheeks have gained my whole affections. I think of when you'll be my wife. Pete and Danny send their regards. They were taken by you I am most certain and probly wish that you were a twin or triplet born . . . All my bubs in the platoon are fine fellows. We joke and tease and take care of one another. So don't worry about me. They are here in your place, pretty puss . . . The most feared guerillas in these parts are named Jessee's guerillas. This is true. My chums are constantly jawing about it . . .*

*Yours*
*Jesse*

\*\*\*\*

*53<sup>rd</sup> KY Rgt. Co.B*
*Oct 29 1864*

*Ma & Pa*
*Glad we're not in the hog trade. What a sorry lot. I*
*can tell you now that is how the army operates . . .*
*My responsibilities suit me. I have no problems with*
*the boys. It's chain of command. I know what's*
*expected of me. They know what's expected of*
*them. . . My sergeant is an upright fellow. Name's*
*Robert Blackwood. He's no harder on me than you*
*ever were, Pa.*
*Overseeing fatigue duty is the worst of my duties.*
*Corporal of the Guard the most important. You would*
*be proud hearing me barking commands . . . Riding*
*on patrol is the most satisfying. Pretty is a true*
*sweetheart.*
*I could use some underdrawers like you make, Ma.*
*The army's make me itch.*

*Your son*
*JJ Cook*

\*\*\*\*

*Ripley, Ohio*
*Nov 5, 1864*

*Dearest Jesse,*

*I will cry whenever I care to. You do not know how lonely it is here. I pine for you. There's only old men cripples and boys to offer a girl compny . . . Work, work, work is all I do. I'm working all the time whilst your out prancing round on that horse. I would love to go to a party or dance.*

*You remember Sallie from down the road? I know you do. You admired her red red hair. Poor Sallie is in a family way. She is not wed and mother says she was laid upon by a soldier. I am not in a family way, dearest Jesse. That is good for you. Papa might shoot you with your fancy army rifle if he knew how you . . .*

*I've heard tell of the Col Jessee you are teased about. He captured a Revenue man from Covington and stole 500 dollars . . .*

*I do fret about you, my Jesse. Every day I fret, and I'm scared of the rumors of Rebels coming cross the river. I saw so many Rebel prisoners passing thro Cincinnati when I went there with the Allenders. Oh, Jesse, you must be careful. I know you must fight to protect us but I could not bear it if . . . like my Uncle Samuel you did not return . . . Mama still mourns for him.*

*When you get back, Jesse. How soon will we get married? What do you think we would call our firstborn? Sallie likes Herman. Herman after her awful grandfather . . .*

*Your sweetheart*
*Liza*

\*\*\*\*

*Covington November 6th 1864*

*Jesse,*
*I wisht I was old enough to be in the army. But even if I looked 18, which I don't, Pa wouldn't sign for me . . . All I do is work . . .*
*Did you hear that the Rebel Genl Hood is going to move into Kentucky? And they're saying that Forrest has taken over Paducah. Where is Paducah? Are you near there?*
*That gorilla Jessee has been stealin' horses around here. I'm supposin' he wouldn't try to stel your horses. You boys would shoot him sure. I wish I had a rifle just in case they do come. Did you hear they might come up through Virginia capture Pittsburg and then come right down the river to Cincinnati?*
*Pa and Uncle Henry say to pay no mind to rumors. I say if there ain't no truth to it, why are you out there in the army?*

*Your brother*
*Theo Cook*

\*\*\*\*

*Covington Kentucky*
*November 10 1864*

*My Dearest Son*

*The days pass. On every one I think of you and worry. Yet I know you are where you should be. We are proud of you, Jesse.*

*Even the grocer Mahoney brags on you. He will never forget you foiling his burglary. I must share all my news with him . . . Mrs. Mahoney writes this for me.*

*Your brothers miss you, even little Willie. I sense it. He probably misses you tossing him up in the air. He did laugh out loud for you . . .*

*News of Uncle Frank is good. He is in New Orleans. So far away. There is no fighting there. They occupy that city.*

*The business is improving sum since trade restrictions are lifting. Your father is working very hard and driving Theo. He will not say no to any work. Henry even stopped by to give him a hand.*

*These times are strange. Strange things going on. A woman gurrilla named Sue Mundy and her men have been murdering Union men near Midway. Imagine that, Jesse. A woman! And there are women criminals right here in Covington. The paper warns that a group of women are posing as relatives of lost soldiers going door to door asking for money.*

*The worst for me is seeing refugees from the south. Last Saturday over four hundred arrived. They look so wretched. The military authorities are taking care of them the best they can.*

*End this, Jesse. Do what you can to end this.*

*I love you.*
*Ma*

# CHAPTER 8

**Lair's Station**
**Four Miles South of Cynthiana, Kentucky**
**Late October, 1864**

They had come upon the train from the east, alerted by smoke belching into the morning sky. Despite the gathering gloom of approaching weather, the plume was distinctive. It was the smoke of a stopped locomotive, but in a place where no locomotive should have stopped.

Sergeant Blackwood, Jesse, and ten of their men pushed the horses in the direction of the smoke. It was rough going; overland, across ditches, through woods.

Finally getting clear of the trees, Jesse made a quick reconnaissance of the scene. The train had been stopped by all too common Rebel blockading of the tracks, but this time the guerrillas had apparently attacked, too.

Men, women, even children were sprawled along the edges of the rail line. Some appeared to be wounded. There was blood. Children were crying, and one female passenger was outright hysterical.

The wounded were being tended to by a man who appeared to be a doctor, along with the train conductor and a few women. Passengers were peering from the windows of the cars. Others were nearly falling out in an effort to get a better view. People were entering and exiting the train at will. But there was no sign of the enemy.

The approach of the horsemen, with pistols raised, caught everyone's attention. The shrieking and crying increased.

"Nooo!"

"Them's more comin'."

"Colonel," someone bellowed.

*Colonel?* Jesse thought.

"No more," a woman cried out. "Oh, Blessed Lord, No!"

"Quiet! They're our boys. Union."

Sensing no danger, Jesse reined in his horse, holstered his pistol and dismounted. Blackwood was right beside him. They knew full well that the rest of the platoon would remain mounted, rifles or revolvers in hand.

"Sergeant, Corporal." A man, obviously in command but dressed in civilian clothes, glared at the two of them. "I'm Colonel Stanhope, 55th Kentucky. You've arrived too late."

"Sir," said Blackwood, "53rd Kentucky. Our apologies, Sir. We came as soon as we sensed the need."

"There's nothing you can do for us here. The situation, in spite of what you see, is under control. We will shortly be backing up to Cynthiana and returning to Covington." He paused, as if considering his options. "Where's your lieutenant?"

"With another platoon from the company, Sir. He could be along at any minute."

"Sergeant, I need you and your men to leave here at once in pursuit of our attackers. You're outnumbered and they've a head start, but they're walking with prisoners. Men of mine. Find them."

"Yes, Sir." Blackwood and Jesse both saluted, hastily remounted, and barked out orders as they circled around to take the lead positions in the patrol.

****

It was impossible to gallop down the uneven roadbed of a rail line without endangering the horses or themselves, so progress was slow. For a mile or two they stayed near the tracks, vigilant, arms at the ready, but they saw no one. Heard nothing.

"They could be anywhere," Jesse said.

"I'm thinking that they would have hightailed it into the woods," remarked Pete. "Where some others might have been waiting."

"I'm thinking the same."

Sergeant Blackwood halted the patrol. "Jesse, whadaya think about splitting up and scouting through the woods? One of us on each side of the tracks?"

Jesse allowed a puff of air to roll across his lips. "We'll each have less men. There's good and bad to that, I suppose. Less easy to detect us, more ground that we can cover, but fewer men to stand and fight."

"Let's do it." The sergeant unfolded his map, sharing it with Jesse. "We'll meet up again here." He tapped the paper. "Look for everything when you ride in there, Jesse. Any sign of horses or people passing through. Anything. And good luck."

"Wish I'd a done some tracking back home," replied Jesse. "Cooperin' didn't much prepare me for this."

Blackwood laughed softly as he reined his horse to turn. "Me, neither. I was a storekeeper."

\*\*\*\*

Jesse's squad picked their way through the woods, hoping in vain for a trail to follow, settling instead for what was possible, following the compass in their designated search area, seeking out small clearings, stretches of sparser growth. He looked at his pocket watch. Time was dragging. The air felt heavy. *Thirty minutes more,* he thought. *Then we got to circle back and meet Blackwood, whether we found anything or not.*

"We're back at the river, Corporal," announced Joe. The woods were indeed beginning to brighten, the land gradually sloping to the banks of the Licking.

"Do we cross it, Jesse?" said Danny.

"Nah, we're just getting farther and farther away from the train with no idea of where they went."

"What are we going to do?"

Jesse still held his watch in his hand. "We're going to stay to the woods. We'll head back to the tracks, just keep a little more to the south . . ."

The words were interrupted by the unexpected sound of distant voices. A group of men began to stumble into sight, following the river—directly towards his small band of soldiers.

Jesse signaled for silence, hoping that his patrol had not been spotted. They backed their horses into the shadow of the trees, drew their firearms, and waited.

"On my command," he whispered. "Joe, Danny, and I will ride out to meet them. You other three, remain here. They will not know how many we are. If shootin' starts, keep a fire from hell coming out of the woods."

The men drew closer. Jesse observed that they were civilians, or at least dressed like civilians. Disheveled. A couple were limping. One fell and was helped to his feet. They looked tired, perhaps physically beaten.

*These fellows could be the men from the train,* he thought, *but where are the Rebs? Did they just let them go? Are their captors somewhere watching us? How in tarnation do I find out?*

Jesse signaled to his men to keep their guns silent as he raised his. His revolver exploded, sending a bullet ricocheting across the dirt and rocks several yards in front of the approaching men. It was unexpected and loud, producing maximum effect.

"Protect yourselves."

"Seek cover, men."

"Don't fire."

"We're not armed, for the love of God."

Jesse stayed alert. He was on edge, fearful of an ambush or trap. The civilians had scrambled for the protection of nearby rocks, or crawled towards the woods edge. There was no return fire.

"If they're out there—the Rebs—we've got to draw them out," Jesse muttered. "Pete, guard the rear." Jesse felt his gut turning. Beads of sweat irritated his lips. With no free hand to wipe them dry, he aimed his revolver. Two more rounds smashed into the rocks and ripped through the dirt.

"Who fires, Sir?" The question was shouted by one of the crouching men, a man who sounded accustomed to wielding authority.

After allowing a few long moments to pass, Jesse called out in what he hoped was his most commanding voice. "Identify yourselves."

Without attempting to rise, the man did so. "Blair is the name. We were taken from a southbound train. Covington to . . ."

"We have been to the train," said Jesse, still in the cover of the shadows. "Where are Everett and his men?"

"They beat us . . . took our weapons, money, watches . . . then skedaddled. They're nowhere to be seen."

"Fuck," muttered Jesse. "I've got to believe them. No other choice." He glanced at both Danny and Joe. "Let's go, boys. Don't let down your guard."

The three front troopers stepped their horses out from the cover of the trees, arms still at the ready. The stillness was palpable. "Corporal Cook, 53rd Kentucky, Union Army, at your service, Sirs."

"Praise be to God!"

"I thought you were going to kill us."

"Just take us outta here!"

Several of the men rose to their feet, hands in the air, so there would be no doubt as to their intentions. "Into the woods," Jesse gestured. "It's best not to hang out here in the open."

****

"Pete Everett and his guerrillas did not know who they had," Jesse said as he related news of the patrol to Stu. They were walking back from a nightly briefing of the regimental non-commissioned officers. Jesse pulled his jacket tighter around him, the cool evening autumnal air hinting of winter. "That fellow Blair was the Ex-Postmaster General of the United States. He's an important official. Everett could've gotten a ransom for him, and some of those fellows in civilian clothes were soldiers from the 55th, put on that train along with some general just to thwart an attack."

"Too bad they didn't. How many did you say was wounded?"

"Ten. Nobody killed, though. The Rebs were shooting at everybody, right into the passenger cars, even at women and children." He stopped, looking directly at Stu, to accentuate the point. "It wasn't very easy getting those fellows back here, neither, without horses, a wagon, nothin'. We put the weakest of 'em on our mounts and walked beside them. When we met up with the sergeant we sent a couple troopers back to camp for help. For mounts and a wagon."

"Sounds like you handled it well. Maybe you'll get a commendation." Stu gave Jesse a warm pat on the soldier.

"Commendation?" Jesse laughed. "All I got was the task of completing a report, a very long report." He glanced into the distant sky, as if to foretell the weather. "I just hope I spelled most of the words right."

# CHAPTER 9

**Camp at Cynthiana, Kentucky
November, 1864**

*The gun exploded. Fire rained. Jesse slashed out with his free hand. He barked a command. Unintelligible. His legs were mired in quicksand. He could not act. Neither advance nor retreat. "No, no." Searing pain. His leg in a vise, twisting, twisting. Fire and blood. Unable to return fire . . .*

A cramp flashed through Jesse's calf muscle, waking him with a start. Daylight had yet to crack the darkness. There was little to see, the faint outline of other cots, the chill cast of the moon beyond the shuttered window. He sat upright, massaging the cramp away. The dream still vivid.

*I should sleep more*, he thought. *God knows what time it even is.*

"Shit," he muttered, feeling nature's call. "'M awake now."

He swung his legs over the edge of the cot, yanked on his boots, and grabbed his jacket. It was cold in the room, nothing in the stove but spent fuel. He gingerly picked his way to the door as not to waken the others, heading outside, where it was colder still.

There was little activity in camp. A few guards on duty. The camp cooks. *If they're up*, he thought, *it's growing near dawn.*

"Can't sleep, Corporal?" The lieutenant had appeared around a corner, possibly making his own way from the latrine.

"Just woke, Sir. I was sleeping poorly. Leg cramps."

"Ah. Sometimes that happens. Too long on a horse, perhaps. Nary any sense in bedding back down now. Reveille's not far off."

"I agree, Sir. Thought I'd go to the mess, maybe beg a cup of coffee."

"Good luck. They can be an ornery crew."

Jesse saluted, having it returned in kind.

He felt in his jacket pocket as he walked. The letter was still there. It would be nice to sit down with a cup of coffee in the warm mess and finish what he had started—a letter to his Pa—and to finish it before the bugler stirred the camp to life.

It was proving difficult to write, and it shouldn't have been. Jesse was usually adept at words, saying just enough to keep the home folks satisfied. But lately, since the train patrol, since the dreams began, convincing words were harder to come by. He felt uneasy.

****

The coffee grew cold in his cup, the words on the page awkward and stiff.

*We're going south. I don't know much on where. Shouldn't tell you if I did.*

Jesse scratched through the few lines he had written, frustrated, all too aware of why he couldn't write.

He wanted to write about the dream. He wanted to know if he was a coward for fearing the gunfire, fearing a bloody battle, fearing what might have happened if the Rebel guerrilla band had indeed been in the woods that day. He wanted to ask if his Pa had ever felt his gut churn in fear, and how his Pa had made it stop. Or, did it ever stop?

He remembered his Pa's words about nothing glorious about killing a man. Had his father killed a man? Had he watched men die? There had been rumors, always rumors about violence and Riley. His father had been in the state penitentiary, for God's sake, a violent place full of violent men. Violent guards.

He had seen his father's temper flare like the exploding gun in his dreams. He felt his father would come out on top in any fight. But would his son?

There was much Jesse wanted to ask, but he would talk of it to no one. Not Pa. Not Uncle Henry, Stu, Pete. No one. He would not dare speak of it, for he could not abide the sense of weakness.

Jesse ripped the paper into shreds as reveille sounded.

# PART THREE

# A DUTIFUL SOLDIER

# CHAPTER 10

**Knoxville, Tennessee**
**December 9, 1864**

Major General George Stoneman pulled all six-feet-four-inches of his powerful frame from the desk chair to stare yet again from the headquarters window. His craggy, field-worn face would reveal no emotion to onlookers. His eyes, however, sparked with determination.

This expedition would be his redemption. Recently, he had been given the command of all the cavalry in Northeastern Tennessee, replacing General Burbridge in that department. The knowledge that Stoneman's abilities were scorned by most of the elite in the officer corps of the Army of the Potomac burned within him like a smoldering torch. It fueled him now, priming him for redemption.

General Hooker had made him a scapegoat with accusations and insinuations that Stoneman was one of the principal reasons for the Union defeat at Chancellorsville. *My God,* thought Stoneman, *Hooker understood nothing about the strategic value of cavalry in that battle. A scapegoat, indeed, for that man's own stupidity and blundering.*

General Sherman's abuse after the Atlanta Campaign was just as damaging to Stoneman's reputation. Stoneman had been the highest-ranking officer to become a prisoner of war, and had spent three months in Confederate custody before Grant arranged for his exchange.

*Sheer humiliation. That's what they've heaped on me—a West Point man, not some store clerk. They'll see what I'm capable of.*

Throughout his ordeals, whenever an allegation from a fellow general had been leveled against him, one man had defended him, Major General John Schofield. It was to Schofield that he had taken his plan for a raid into Virginia. "I can lick Breckenridge," Stoneman had told him, "if given an opportunity." Schofield had reviewed the plan, made some amendments of his own, and unleashed Stoneman and his cavalrymen to seek the objective which had eluded Burbridge.

Stoneman's gaze swept the expanse of activity evident beyond the headquarters building. He would resurrect his reputation during these waning months of the war. Five thousand five hundred horsemen, wagons, artillery units, materiel, and supplies in various stages of readiness were preparing to march on his command.

"Major." He beckoned to his aide who had been waiting quietly near the door. "It's time."

Almost instantaneously the room began to fill. They had merely been waiting in the hallway, in an adjacent room, Stoneman's staff officers and field commanders. *Waiting, as well it should be,* thought Stoneman.

He nodded at his second-in-command, Brigadier General Alvan Gillem, who was in the process of handpicking 1,500 troopers from the ranks of those assembled to be his lead force. He begrudgingly acknowledged Brigadier General Stephen Burbridge, who had traveled through the Cumberland Gap with his division of 4,200 cavalrymen, which included the 5th and 6th U.S. Colored Cavalry Regiments. *Ah, General Burbridge,* thought Stoneman. *You failed miserably in October and now must watch me accomplish what you could not. How satisfying that will prove to be.*

"Gentlemen," Stoneman said simply, his gaze boring into each of theirs in turn. "The time has come. We will move in the morning."

His aides began to spread out maps of Tennessee and Virginia on the table as the senior officers gathered round.

"Sir!" Burbridge peered at the map of Virginia. "What is our ultimate objective?"

"Patience, General. All will be revealed in good time. Let us stay focused on tomorrow. How go the preparations of your division?"

\*\*\*\*

Sergeant Blackwood and Corporal Perry had laid out two large blankets in front of the men of Company B. On each blanket lay small piles of sugar and coffee beans. There was no practical way to divvy a ration of loose coffee and sugar equitably, so they dumped the coveted goods into equal-looking piles as best they could and called the men randomly to advance and take a share.

Today Blackwood was using the every fourth man technique, reading from the company roster and then repeating until all men were called. "Evans, Justice, Krimmelbein, Sommerkamp . . ."

Jesse looked on. His share was already stowed in his haversack, a small privilege of rank. He noted that most of the men did as he did, immediately mixing the beans with the sugar. Soldiers loved their coffee sweet, their only sweet while on the march.

One by one his squad gathered around him: Krimmelbein, West, Strong, Grubbs, and Appel. "Each of you will be issued five days' rations, one day's forage of corn, and four horseshoes with nails, to go along with the 63 rounds of ammunition we already carry. Looks like before this is over we may be pressed to forage and live off the land. If'n the supply wagons don't keep pace." Jesse paused in his monologue, turning to survey the mass of men and activity around them. "Let's get going, make the rounds of the cracker lines, and pack up. Lieutenant says we're moving in the morning."

"But I like Knoxville," groused Grubbs, "Did you get a look at some of these Southern girls?"

"What girls?" said Pete, slapping him on the back of the head as they started to walk. "You must've been dreaming. All I've seen is horses, guts, a mule or two, and some old cows we ain't supposed to eat."

"Maybe Johnny thought the old cows were girls," added West. "He's been outta Covington a long time now."

"Only girls I've seen since leaving Kentucky could be cows," said Jesse. "Skinny, homely ones at that."

"That's because you're swooning over Eliza, Corporal Cook. Woman's got her hooks in you deep." Pete grinned at his chum.

"Never shoulda introduced you."

They filed into a line for the first of their rations, bunching together in conversation.

"Is it a fact, Corporal, that the 53$^{rd}$ is gonna be Burbridge's front regiment?" asked Appel.

"Don't ask me things I'm not privy to, Charley."

"Or ain't obliged to tell," retorted Pete.

"If we are up front," Jesse continued, "it's an honor, I suppose. We must have impressed somebody with our riding." He smiled, enjoying his own joke.

"What I figure," said Pete, "is that I impressed somebody."

"Shut it, Pete."

"God Ahmighty," muttered Danny. "The front regiment, first to get shot at."

"Won't be no need for shootin', West. Your ugly face'll scare the sons-of-bitches to death before we can take aim," taunted Pete.

*Still at it,* thought Jesse, shaking his head. *Pete.*

"Boys," he said aloud. "Even if we are Burbridges's front regiment, which I doubt, all of us will be behind General Gillem's division."

Stu and the remainder of the platoon had joined them in line.

"I overheard you, Corporal," said Stu. "Personally, I think the coloreds will be the lead regiments. They're regular army, not state, and them being up front will make a statement throughout these parts."

# CHAPTER 11

## On the Road to Kingsport, Tennessee
## December 1864

*"Hard times are a-comin', comin'..."* Jesse's fine baritone seemed to drift skyward in the smoke from the now-dying campfire, Stu accompanying him on mouth organ. They had sung several Stephen Foster songs, preferring those to the army tunes they knew.

"You two make pretty music. Sure do," commented Blackwood. "I never knew you were a singer, Jesse."

"Sing all the time. Must run in the family. Somebody's always singin' or whistlin' at our place." He shifted his position on the rock upon which he was sitting—a futile attempt to absorb more heat from the fire.

"I miss them," said Danny.

"My folks?" teased Jesse.

"My own. You know what I mean."

Jesse chuckled, giving Danny a nudge with his boot. "Especially his grandmother. Danny's grandmama really favors our boy."

"That's a nice thing," offered Blackwood. "I think I was my ma's favorite. She'd never say for sure. It certainly wasn't my brother Emmor." Laughter circled the flames. "Gotta 'nother log for this fire, Charley? Anybody?"

"You know anymore songs, Jesse, Stu?"

"Did *Beautiful Dreamer* already. What about *Gentle Annie*?" replied Jesse.

"Could you pick a sadder one?" said Pete huskily. He had just awakened after drifting off to sleep.

"Not as sad as that." Stu gestured into the darkness. "I've been hearin' them off and on all evening. What are they singing?"

"Negro spirituals," said Blackwood. "That's some of the colored cavalry camped over there."

Jesse softly sang a line familiar to them all. "*I hear those gentle voices calling Old Black Joe . . .*"

A damper seemed to settle over their easy banter. Most in the circle glanced towards the distant campfire and listened to the plaintive sounds.

"I'll never get used to seeing colored soldiers ridin' right alongside us," growled Pete.

"I guess that's why we're here, boys," said Blackwood. "Times are a'changing."

Pete grunted. "I'm a Union man. That's why I'm here." He looked around. "Nobody on the bridge wanted coloreds workin' long side 'im." When there was little response, he pushed. "What about you, Jesse?"

Jesse slowly rubbed his now-bristly chin. "I'm a Unionist, too, Pete, but it's more than that with me. I have family in Ripley, Ohio. Tarnation, you went there with me. Ripley's a sanctuary for escaped slaves. It's where they head for when they cross the river into the North. There's a house on the hill that shines a light." He paused, deciding how much to say. "I've seen some pitiful, wretched coloreds . . . I wouldn't want to be them. If I was them I'd be over there now, ridin' in that regiment."

"So, you're an abolitionist," remarked Stu.

"Let's put it this way, Stu. My younger brother, his name is Theodore Parker Cook. You know who Theodore Parker is?"

"I do," said Blackwood. "Preacher from New England. Abolitionist. Lincoln used some of his quotes in his speeches. That does speak loudly about your family, Corporal."

Jesse spoke quietly, staring into the fire. "Parker said that we are all members of a great army achieving the welfare of the world. That we all must do our duty, whether it's in the shop, the kitchen, market, or school. Even in the front rank of some great battle. It's our *duty*."

# CHAPTER 12

**Bean's Station, Tennessee**
**December 12, 1864**

Another temporary headquarters. They had been on the march for three days. Major General Stoneman pointed his stick at the far southwestern region of the State of Virginia. "Saltville, Gentlemen. That is our ultimate objective."

Nods of understanding and quiet comment traveled through his officer corps as they finally grasped their mission. Only General Burbridge, who had been in command mere months earlier when Saltville was not taken, stood stoically silent.

"We will destroy the saltworks, depriving the Southern army, indeed the Southern populace, of their last bastion for food preservation," Stoneman continued. "Along the way, our boys will destroy everything: the lead mines, the rail lines, anything of value in pivotal towns such as Kingsport, Bristol, Abingdon, Glade Spring, Wytheville, and Marion." He stabbed each town on the map as if to pierce its heart, the towns he would raid with his well-equipped, formidable cavalry.

"We shall bring the Confederacy to its knees, Gentlemen, by depriving it of its muscular and skeletal structure."

## Kingsport, Tennessee
## December 13, 1864

Jesse slouched deeper into the saddle. After three days of riding through the mountains in frigid winter weather, he had about enough of soldiering. His great coat did little to push back the cold, especially at night. The bivouacs had been brutal— too cold for easy conversation or singing 'round a fire. The feet. The hands. They were proving especially difficult to keep warm.

The army was stopping, massing near the western bank of the Holston River. Jesse would learn that later, as well as the name of the town he saw on the other shore, Kingsport.

"Are there Rebs in that town, Corporal? Do you think?"

"We'll know soon enough, Charley." Jesse had seen the lieutenant ride off, presumably for orders. He would return shortly, call his non-commissioned officers together, and then thy would know. In the meantime, they stayed mounted.

"My opinion is, they know we're here," Jesse said. "Not much movement over there. Waiting."

"That bridge is crap," said Pete. "Won't be crossin' that. It's about ready to pitch into the river. I don't think I could crawl across that bridge. No way my horse could do it."

Blackwood walked his horse beside Jesse's. "Lieutenant's back, Corporal. Let's go."

They formed a semi-circle facing the lieutenants and Captain Haggerty: Blackwood, four other sergeants, Jesse, Stu, six more corporals. The men who would lead Company B.

"Part of our force will remain here," the captain said, "as a diversion. The enemy is probably confident in their position, fortified in a manner of speaking behind that dilapidated bridge. They know we can't cross easily in a frontal attack. However, our scouts have located a ford, roughly three miles upstream. Our job, Men, is to cross the river at the ford, make our way down the eastern bank, and God willing, surprise the Rebs with one Hell of a flank attack. Two regiments will be on the move, including ours. We leave immediately." He paused. "Any questions?" When there appeared to be none, he simply said, "Then see to your men."

\*\*\*\*

They had located the ford and crossed the river without incident, preparing to ride into Kingsport. But the scouts had come thundering back to the lead riders. An entire Confederate supply train had been spotted exiting the town. Lightly guarded, a definite prize. It would be easy enough for Stoneman's raiders to overtake it.

The front regiment split into two contingents, a flanking maneuver practiced countless times. They rode at a moderate gallop, on the road when possible and cross-country when necessary, guided competently by the cadre of scouts. After crossing a rock-hard field and yet another icy stream, Company B stood on the crest of a rise staring down at the hapless wagon train. Not far in the distance they could see the other half of the regiment, forming to attack from another direction. Hundreds of men, armed and ready.

*Surely, they'll just surrender,* thought Jesse. *They've no chance. The loads those horses are bearing.*

But the Rebel teamsters and their guard had other ideas. Upon catching sight of the Union soldiers, the wagoners spurred their teams onward. Mounted guards wheeled to face the attackers. Marksmen posted inside braced their rifles on wagon sides and backboards. Guards seated next to drivers cocked their guns as well. The initial shots came from Southern rifles.

****

At the bugle's command, Jesse spurred Pretty down the rise, his revolver cocked and held high, the cape of his great coat flapping in the wind. He preferred the Colt revolver to either the carbine rifle or his saber when on horseback.

"Relax," he said to himself. "Trust the horse. Trust Pretty. Check your position. Stay in control."

Jesse had shot at men before, perhaps even wounded one as they skedaddled into the woods, those marauding bands of guerrillas. It was hard to tell whose shot felled a man, though, whose aim drove true. Jesse had never shot a man at point blank range, and he had rarely been shot at. He would not allow himself to think on that now.

"Pete. Charley. Danny. Joe," Jesse bellowed. "Let's drive. Keep your heads. Stay together." The time for thinking was past. It was time for action, for relying on training and gut instinct.

Jesse set his horse on a parallel track with a wagon about mid-way down the jostling train. He heard the whiz of a bullet slash past his head. Another. Hooves thundered behind and past him.

*Don't think. Act!*

Mere seconds passed, but time seemed eternal. His world reduced to sounds and sensations. The sickening thud of a horse breaking down. Cursing. Screams. The metallic screeching of braking wheels. Wood splintering. Crashes. Gunfire. The uncontrollable churning of his gut.

He sensed the wagoner's guard reloading his weapon.

*Shoot him first!* The words screamed in Jesse's head.

Jesse paced his horse to match the speed of the wagon. Drawing near the wagon seat, he fired, into the startled face of the Rebel guard. The revolver spit fire and smoke, its force jerking back Jesse's hand.

The wagon began careening out of control, for someone else had brought down the wagoner. Jesse pulled Pretty deftly from the melee, caught sight of Pete and hastened to regroup with his squad.

The entire wagon train was slowing. Stopping. Beleaguered teamsters reined in their frightened teams. A scrap of cloth fluttered from a musket. Southern hands mournfully pierced the air.

"Good work, Corporal, Boys. We've quite the prize." Their lieutenant had stopped to praise them, and then just as quickly moved on.

"Relieved to see you all in one piece," Jesse said, a shudder coursing through his tensed body.

"Shit. I didn't even fire my gun," said Danny. "Too few of them to shoot at, and I'll be damned if I'm gonna shoot some helpless horse."

"I saw you, Jesse." Pete spoke quietly as their mounts pulled head to head. "You're a ruthless son-of-a-bitch. Long ways from our alley fight. Impressive."

"Just doin' my duty, Pete." Jesse took a long swig from his canteen—his mouth so dry. "No more'n choppin' the head off one of Ma's chickens."

"Well, Mama's Boy, you got the chicken's blood and guts all over you."

Jesse looked at his leg, at the hem of his coat. They were splattered with blood and pieces of . . . He had not seen the soldier's face explode as the body fell towards him. He had seen the face, twisted in fear and loathing, as he aimed his revolver. But once the trigger was pulled he saw only the gun—fire and smoke.

He felt nausea, his stomach starting to turn. "Beat it down," he muttered. "Put it out of yer mind." Looking again at Pete, he did not speak. Jesse simply spurred his horse to follow the now departing column, which was heading to Kingsport to assault from the rear its Rebel defenders.

He felt colder still, considering his father's cautionary words and what lie ahead. Bending over in his saddle, he laid his head on Pretty's neck and vomited. Still retching, he straightened back up, wiped his mouth with his sleeve and reached for his canteen.

# CHAPTER 13

## Southwestern Virginia

Jesse was in a black mood. His squad was on foraging duty, and in his mind that was nothing short of thievery. *Excuse me, M'am. I'm going to take your last hog here on behalf of the United States Army. No matter that you won't be able to feed your young'uns . . . God, is this what bein' a soldier is? Stealing supplies from women and children?* He couldn't help but think of his own mother and younger brothers, cringed at the thought of strange soldiers barging into his home, demanding at gunpoint whatever his ma might have. He was ready to be done with it, take the sacks of dried and preserved foods they had slung over their horses and head back to camp.

"Leave me alone . . . No!" The girl screamed.

The man struck her a second time, all the time maintaining his grip. "You be quiet, Gal. Whole damned South'll hear ya."

Her faint, but unmistakably anguished cry caught the attention of Jesse and Pete, who were in the lead, riding side by side up a narrow, rutted lane.

Jesse halted the squad with a hand signal, and motioned to his left into the woods. "It's comin' from over there." Without taking his eyes from the stand of trees, he pulled his Colt revolver from its holster and cocked it. "We can't just ignore her."

"She's probly just wailin' because somebody wants to take her cow," said Pete.

"Or somethin', else," replied Jesse.

"Fuck it, we're not musketeers, rescuing damsels in distress . . . Not worth gettin' shot at."

Jesse glared at him, then urged his horse forward. Pete scoffed, but followed without hesitation, as did the other four riders.

They beat their way through the trees, pushing aside low-hanging branches, or ducking beneath them. Jesse knew they had mere minutes before their presence would be revealed. Devoid of foliage, the winter woods loomed open and bare, not an easy place to approach unannounced. Their only hope would be coming upon whomever it was from behind, but there was no way of knowing.

"I ain't got nothin' for you." A girl, maybe fifteen or sixteen, thrashed her arms wildly at a dismounted Union corporal who had her in his burly grasp. Several privates stood nearby, snickering.

"I'm thinkin' you do, Missy," the soldier sneered. "You Rebs all got stuff buried. And, if'n you don't, well, you can make it up to me." He groped the girl's breast. "Real pretty. So soft."

Thoughts of Eliza, in the stable, in his arms flashed in Jesse's memory. "Leave her alone, or I'll kill you."

The startled corporal spun around at the sound of Jesse's menacing voice, releasing the girl as he did so. He had not heard the footfalls of the horses. He had heard nary a neigh nor the cocking of a firearm, so intent was he on the girl, who had now staggered into the woods. Out of sight.

The corporal, not from the 53$^{rd}$, found himself staring into the barrel of Jesse's revolver which was leveled at his head. "Well, now," he was stunned. "You're Union, not some Secesh. You're one of us. Let's reconsider this, Corporal. One to another. Corporal . . . who?"

"Cook," Jesse said. "And there's nothin' to reconsider."

"Corporal Cook," drawled the man unctuously. "We was just having a little fun. Nothin' for you to get all upset about. Weren't we, Boys?" He looked from Jesse to the privates accompanying him. "We're all one and the same. Your boys, my boys. Out foraging for Uncle Sam. They ordered us to take what we could find. We found that little wench. You'd a done the same."

*You son of a bitch,* Jesse thought. *You rotten son of a bitch.*

Jesse did not lower his arm. He did not flinch or avert his gaze. Moments passed. The unknown corporal began to grow uncomfortable, began to squirm under Jesse's relentless stare.

Finally, Jesse spoke. "I'm not the likes of you, Corporal." He spat out the word. "Never will be. You're a disgrace. Now get the hell out of here before I change my mind about shooting you." He flexed his arm, pointed the Colt into the air and fired.

The wayward soldiers quickly retreated to their horses, not daring to look back as they rode away. Jesse noticed that every one of his own men was holding a pistol or rifle, even Pete.

"I wouldn't have let him kill you, if it came to that, Corporal. In fact, I wanted to bust his ugly face," said Pete, watching the perpetrators ride off. "We shoulda thrashed 'em."

"And been brought up on charges?"

"What charges? Their word agin ours."

Jesse yanked on Pretty's reins. "Let's go find the girl."

"Oh, come on, Jesse. She's all right. We should get outta here."

"We'll find the girl." There was no quarrel to be had.

****

It did not take them long. She sat huddled next to a log, her arms wrapped tightly around her legs, whimpering. With her bedraggled hair and dirty and ragged clothes, she reminded Jesse of a cur, a lost and pathetic mutt who'd been kicked one too many times.

He got down slowly from his horse, approaching her the same way he would a frightened animal. He spoke quietly, not attempting to touch her, not moving too close, and he motioned for his squad mates to back away.

"What's your name?"

She tried to shrink even tighter into a ball.

"Where do you live?"

No answer.

"We're not like those other soldiers. They were bad men. We won't hurt you. What's your name?"

She lifted her head slightly. He could see the welt growing on her cheek, the blackened eye.

"What's your name?"

"Effie." She said it so quietly he could barely hear.

"Effie. That's my Gramma's name. You'd like my Gramma." He was closer to her now, squatting down, one knee in the dirt. "You look so cold, Effie. Let me take you home. Somebody's worried 'bout you. I know they are."

"My Grampa."

"Oh." Jesse's heart began to pound. For the first time he realized that he might have made a mistake, might be leading his men into danger. A grandfather to this girl would shoot them on sight. He had no doubt about that.

"Okay, Effie." Jesse stood, sent a pleading look at Pete.

"We can get her close, Corporal. Drop her off. See her safely home, and back out before trouble."

Jesse turned his attention to Effie, who had begun to shake nearly uncontrollably. "You're coming with us, Girl." He scooped her up in his arms, alarmed at how skinny and lightweight she felt. She continued to tremble and cry. "I'm going to put you on my horse, Effie. Her name's Pretty. She'll like you. Then I'm going to sit behind you and keep you from falling. Don't be afraid, Effie. I won't hurt you."

Once in the saddle, his boots firmly in the stirrups, the girl slumping between his arms, Jesse started out. "Show us the way, Effie. We'll get you home."

Pete rode next to Jesse, his pistol loaded and ready. Danny, Joe, Charley, and Johnny spread out, on the lookout for anything suspicious.

****

Jesse didn't know what he expected, but it wasn't this—a ferocious man wielding a pick ax, bellowing like a prophet.

The girl had guided them to a homestead on what looked like an abandoned subsistence farm. It wasn't much of a place. Everything he looked at needed repair, cried out for a man's hand.

The old man was clad in a sack-like garment, as if just arisen from a sick bed. His beard was long, gray, and matted. He stared at the six riders, wild-eyed, and began to stumble down the steps in their direction. Pete fully cocked his pistol.

The click stirred Effie. "Don't shoot him! Let me down!" She clawed at Jesse's arms, and then began thrashing, in a vain attempt to slide off the horse. "Grampa! That's my grandpapa."

"Effie Gentry, is that you? Who you with? Runnin' off again. Satan's kin, you are! Just like your mama."

"Gentry." Jesse spoke his mother's name in a mere whisper, her words resounding in his head. *I was born there, you know. In those Virginia hills . . . cousins of mine. Cousins of yours . . . lying in wait for you . . . You could be fighting our own.*

"Tarnation," Jesse yelled. Effie had gouged his eye in her effort to be free. Recoiling, he nearly threw her to the ground. His eye was watering, his cheek smarting from her fingernails' trailing down its length.

The old man lurched towards them, veering erratically, swinging the ax as he came. As he neared, Jesse noticed the eyes. They looked at nothing. No focus. Vacant. This man was more than deranged. He was sightless. "Pete, don't shoot. The old fella's blind." Jesse had to decide what to do, quickly. "Charley, Danny, ride around the house. Secure the rear. Joe, Johnny, check the barn. Pete, stand by me."

"Sir," Jesse said. "Put down that ax. No one will get hurt. We are returning your granddaughter safe and sound."

"Heathens! The Lord God will have his revenge!" Flailing the pick ax from side to side the man lunged towards the sound of Jesse's voice. It was spooking Pretty. She neighed, backed up, pawed the ground, and then rose on her hind legs, nearly unseating Jesse.

Pete had enough of what he considered sheer nonsense. He spurred his horse towards the elderly man, whacking the ax from the fellow's hand with the butt of his rifle. The sheer force of it knocked the man to the ground.

Effie screamed and threw herself on her grandfather's limp body. "Grandpapa! Oh, Grandpapa." Upon seeing Jesse's boots, who had walked over to see if the old man was alive or dead, she quietly hissed, "I hate all of you."

Jesse grabbed her by the shoulders and hauled her to her feet. "Pete. Bring him inside or he will be dead. I'll take my cousin here."

"Cousin?" Pete said incredulously.

"You ain't no cousin of mine." The girl continued to twist, kick, and thrash at Jesse as he half-walked, half-dragged her into the house. "I never seen you before."

****

The fire Joe had built crackled in the fireplace. Finally, the girl seemed to be recovering her color. The trembling had stopped. The old man breathed heavily, occasionally muttering, in some state of half-sleep. They had heaped anything they could find on top of him to provide warmth. Jesse had given the girl his blanket roll.

"I'm sorry I hurt you," she said.

"'S Okay. You're spirited. I'm sorry I had to be so rough to calm you down."

"We gotta get goin', Corporal," said Pete.

"I know."

"It sure is pleasant just settin' here by the fire, though, idn't it?" remarked Danny.

"Jesse. Do you really think we could be cousins?"

"You got the same name as my ma. Gentry. You got the exact same name as my Gramma, Effie Gentry. My ma was born in Virginia. Moved north when she was young. Married my pa in Ohio. So, yeah." He gestured towards the old man. "Ask him when he revives." Slowly, Jesse got to his feet and reached for his greatcoat. "How will you survive the winter here, Effie? You've nothing."

"I get by."

"How?" Jesse demanded. "What do you eat? Who chops the wood? Where's an able-bodied man around here?" Something in him knew he did not want to hear the answer. The able-bodied men, whoever they were, were dead in the war, or out there still. Waiting.

"I was checkin' my snares. Had a rabbit, too. But they took it."

Jesse rubbed his chin in his hand. "Come with us. We can strap your grandfather to a horse. Surrender to the army. They'll feed you."

"I'll never be a prisoner of war." Her eyes flashed. "I'll die first. What do you think I am?"

"You might just get your wish." Jesse buttoned his coat, reached for his rifle, secured his saber. "Look. The army won't keep you long. They'll release you. You're a kid with a sick old man. You can go north. Make your way to my mother. She'll take care of you, care of him. There's refugees all over my town."

"No."

"What in the name of God are you going to do here while you wait for somebody who may never come back?  What are you gonna eat? Who says the next soldiers that come through here won't do what they . . ."

Effie rose from the stool on which she was sitting and slapped Jesse hard on the cheek she had previously clawed. "Don't talk about kin you do not know. You know NOTHING."

Pete grabbed Jesse's sleeve, "Corporal, we gotta go."

Jesse shoved Pete aside and stormed out the door. Momentarily he returned with two sacks of the supplies they had managed to forage. He threw it at Effie's feet. "Here, take these. They'll do you for a spell. Hide them good."

"Corporal . . ." There was uncertainty in Danny's voice.

"I don't want your stolen goods," spat Effie.

Jesse pounded across the wooden floor. He yanked the door open. Before slamming it in her face, he glared back at her and growled, "Then burn them."

Back on his horse, he scowled at Danny and anyone else who dared question him. "We didn't have a good day of foraging. Understand? Didn't find much at all.  Now, let's ride." He spurred Pretty harder than he meant to. She replied with a whinny and bolted. Tears of anger were welling in his eyes. He needed to be in the lead, far in the lead, away from the others. He smacked Pretty again.

His face and heart smarted from Effie's attack. Her words exploded in his ears, words he did not want to hear. Plus, the beseeching words of his ma: *Do what you can to end this, Son.*

"Damn it. Goddammit," he cried.

# CHAPTER 14

**Abingdon, Virginia**
**December 15, 1864**

Jesse watched the last of his squad remount—their work on this now-destroyed section of the Virginia and Tennessee Railroad accomplished.

The troopers had pried up all the ties and rails from a segment of track. They had thrown the ties into a pile, directly on the roadbed, and then placed the rails on top of the heap. It had been backbreaking work, even with the help of horses.

The ties had been set aflame, and soon the rails glowed red at the centers. To complete the destruction, a few soldiers had dragged one rail off the pile, bent it around a nearby tree, and twisted it. This would only add to the difficulty for any Rebs who attempted to rebuild.

"Sure is an effective way to ruin a railroad," Jesse said.

"First time in three days I haven't been fucking freezing," commented Pete.

"Yeah, between the fire and workin', I have warmed up some."

"My toes are still numb, though," said Charley. "Almost wish I'd have been on that prison detail after we took Kingsport, escorting them Rebs back to Knoxville. I'd be in a building somewhere now. Sleepin' on a cot."

"Shoulda had us forage for blankets, coats, and warmer socks," whined Johnny.

"Sie haben keine," replied Joe. "People's poor here."

"Let's ride," commanded Jesse, spotting Sergeant Blackwood and the remainder of the company forming up. "Our day's not finished." Besides, he had no desire to discuss the living conditions of anyone in these mountains.

They had advanced relentlessly through southwestern Virginia, driving remnants of the Confederate forces before them. They had burned railroad trestles, rolling stock, and depots, meeting little resistance along the way. They'd foraged and raided, heaping destruction on anything or anyone in their way.

Jesse hated everything about it: what he was compelled to do, and the country he was doing it in.

Now, he was galloping into Abingdon, a raider on a mission to destroy and demoralize, along with hundreds of other armed, dirty, tired, cold, wet, mostly young men. Jesse had been surprised to learn that a number of his comrades were mountain boys, from nearby towns and hollows in Kentucky, Tennessee, even Virginia. Throughout the Central

Appalachians men had taken sides, and some had chosen to ride with the Union.

When they entered Abingdon, the few townspeople on the street quickly scrambled for cover. Frightened children clung to their mothers' skirts as the women pulled them into inner rooms of their mostly modest houses. When the rare civilian attempted to stand firm against the invaders, he was summarily whacked with a rifle, saber, or shot. Most people stayed well hidden. Anxious eyes took a furtive peek from a frosted window, only to disappear. The Confederate soldiers, who Jesse had expected to mount some sort of resistance, seemed to evaporate under the pressure of facing Stoneman's cavalry.

The horsemen succeeded at sparking fear. They encircled homes. Discharged guns. Broke windows. Tore down fences. Captured livestock. Stole horses. Burned wagons. Bashed in storefronts. Stripped shelves. Stomped. Ripped. Confiscated. Destroyed.

****

Jesse smashed his foot through the partially open door of the shed, revolver fully cocked, Krimmelbein behind him. He felt only half human, a dirty extension of his horse.

He blinked. Almost startled. This was familiar territory. The adze and other tools of his family's trade. The partially finished barrels, the ready staves, hooping materials. A cooper shop.

A boy no older than his brother Theo, thirteen or so, crouched trembling in a shadowy corner. He was dirtier than Theo would have been, skinnier, pallid.

"Get up," Jesse demanded. "Stand up."

The boy did so slowly, visibly shaking.

"Where's your pa?"

"Somewhere's 'round Richmond probly."

"Your ma here? Older brothers?"

The boy shook his head in the negative, fearful.

"You runnin' the shop?"

"Best I can."

Jesse could scarcely hear him. His thoughts were clouding. Somewhere back in Illinois. He was barely fifteen years old. His own pa, convicted of burglary. The shame he'd felt came flooding back. His own pa, carted off to the jailhouse. And, then, the sentencing: two years in Joliet Prison. Two years in which Jesse would have to fend for his family—alone.

He remembered the man, a customer . . . had come barging into his father's struggling shop. Not knowing the circumstances. Not feeling the embarrassment, nor the anger.

*You runnin' the shop, boy? Don't look n'er strong nor old enough to be cooperin' by yerself. Where's your pa?*

*Ain't got no pa just now, and I know exactly what I'm doing.*

He remembered the fear in his gut. The uncertainty. He remembered saying, *Is there somethin' Cooks can do for you, Sir?* And the derisive laughter in return.

Krimmelbein's voice jolted him back to the present. "Ve gonna burn this place, Jesse? Take these here tools? Some of them looks dangerous."

Jesse stared at the boy. "You workin' that barrel yourself?"

"Yessir." His voice trembled.

"Work ain't bad. Ain't good neither, but it ain't bad." Jesse reached out, touching the barrel with his free hand. "Needs more chiselin' here." He stroked the wood with his fingers. "Angle it a little to the left. It'll give you a tighter seal when..." He stopped, noticing the boy's uncertain expression.

"You a cooper, sir?"

"Was . . . Am."

"Jesse?" Krimmelbein implored.

Jesse continued to touch what felt so familiar beneath his craftsman's hands, gently caressing the rounded beauty of the barrel coming to life under the boy's emerging skill. He saw it all so vividly: his father's cooper shop, the stacked kegs, the unworked wood, the ready staves of various size and thickness, the aprons, caps, and dusty boots, the tools, sharpeners, stove, cabinets, the stools, buckets, workbenches and piles of hoops. The sweet aroma of wood.

*Was a cooper . . . Am a soldier,* he thought. He shook his head, not wanting to remember any of it. Especially not wanting to remember that night in the alley. He had heaped such righteous distain on

Rebel sympathizers who were committing far less of an evil deed than he was capable of now.

*Do your duty.* He felt confused, angry, and so very tired. Too tired to sort it out. He only knew that, duty or no duty, he could not harm this boy so like himself.

Jesse jammed the revolver back in his holster, not taking his eyes off the boy. "You need to skedaddle. There has to be a back way outta here." Putting his hand in his haversack he tossed the boy some hardtack. "When we leave, you git. And don't come back until all the horsemen are gone."

He then swung around to face Krimmelbein. "Joe, let's go. There's more important prizes than this."

Krimmelbein had no qualms with Jesse's decision. They remounted. Spurring Pretty into the street, Jesse took one glance backward towards the shed.

"Theo. . ."

\*\*\*\*

It looked to Jesse like his mates had gone foraging when he met up with the rest of the squad. Danny had been with Jesse and Joe, posted outside the cooper shop. The others, though, had split off under directions from Blackwood. They were in a rowdy mood, and Jesse was thankful that all of them had not been with him. They would have observed his every action, perhaps found him lacking. His own

Pa's words were seared in his brain. *"He's not the type."*

*Not the type for what, Pa? Not the type who likes to kill? Not the type who likes to steal, pilfer, and burn?* He bit his lower lip and took a deep breath. *Enough of this. We've a war to fight.*

Reports quickly spread through the regiment that Confederate partisans were on their tail, had entered the town. The sound of repeated gunfire seemed to bear that out. Troops were on the move. Bugles sounded. Jesse waved his men forward, as did Blackwood, and Stu, who had ridden up behind them, his own squad in tow.

They thundered out of Abingdon at a gallop, the sun already setting in the winter sky. The hour was not late, but it was nearing the shortest day of the year. At a safe distance they drew up. Scouts had found a suitable place to bivouac, and they would have to do it in near darkness.

Jesse reined in Pretty to the slowest of walks. He needed orders: where to camp, where to tether the horses. He looked over his shoulder, thinking Blackwood might be there. Instead he caught sight of distant flames illuminating the night sky. "My God," he muttered. "Are we burning the town?"

"Oughta burn the whole damned South," replied an unknown voice. "That would be justice."

"God is the purveyor of justice," remarked Jesse, "not us." He rode off into the darkness, growing cold, even as flames ate at his core.

# CHAPTER 15

**Headquarters**
**Confederate Forces**
**Saltville, Virginia**
**December 16, 1864**


     Major General John C. Breckinridge, former Vice-President of the United States, and now the commander of the Department of Southwest Virginia, CSA, turned his tired eyes once again to the maps lying before him. He addressed his senior officers:  Colonel Henry Giltner, Brigadier General Basil Duke, Brigadier General George Cosby, Colonel Vincent Witcher, and Colonel Robert Preston. The gloom of the headquarters lamp reflected the dismal prospect of what they were about to undertake.

     "We have no choice but to attempt to stem Stoneman's advance," Breckinridge said. "He has wreaked havoc on the railroad, destroyed our supply depot at Abington. He will, no doubt, do the same to our supplies in Wytheville. He has continually beaten back what cavalry we have sent against him. Our scouts currently have him sited just outside Wytheville and the Austinville lead opeations."

"His strength?" asked Cosby.

"We are outnumbered five to one, George. It is grim, Gentlemen, but we will have the element of surprise if we move tonight."

"We also have some of the best men in the south, Sir," offered Basil Duke. "Fine cavalrymen from Virginia and Kentucky. The 11th Kentucky Mounted Rifles. Fine men. Excellent soldiers."

"I do not question the abilities of our men, General. But I believe that in this battle we will also need the hand of Providence."

"Our orders?" asked Witcher.

"We will move from Saltville tonight, with all one thousand regulars. Colonel Preston, you will remain in command of the five hundred militia men we hold in reserve to defend the saltworks. Colonel Witcher you will go ahead of the main force with the 34th Battalion, top speed, and harass the Union forces as much as possible.

"It has rained four inches in the last few days. It won't be an easy ride, Gentlemen. The roads are muddy and difficult. Do the best you can. I expect to be crossing Walkers Mountain with our main force by 3:00 a.m."

## Near Wytheville, Virginia
## December 17, 1864
## Morning


Jesse pulled himself up on one elbow, his hand cradling his chin. Pre-dawn. *It's so fucking cold,* he thought. His bowels were raging. *Flux?* For the third time that night he yanked himself to his feet. He stumbled through the mass of exhausted, slumbering soldiers. Some were snoring. Others mumbled and thrashed about. Some simply lay there, unable to sleep. Wiping his runny nose on an already filthy shirtsleeve, Jesse staggered towards the latrine.

It had been a dreamless sleep, what little he had. Nothing pleasant. Nothing soothing. Just the churning in his gut, coming and going, twisting, twisting, and the all-too-vivid realization that he would spend yet another day in the saddle, with numb fingers and aching feet. It had been two days since their raid on Abingdon and they had been pushing hard, driving the Confederate cavalry before them.

By the time Jesse worked his way back to his platoon, some of the men were stirring. Krimmelbein had stoked the fire. Coffee was brewing.

"You look peaked, about as good as I feel," said Sergeant Blackwood, giving Jesse a feeble smile in greeting.

"Then you must feel like shit."

"Orders are coming down momentarily, Corporal. I wouldn't let the men get too comfortable. It won't be breakfast at mama's kitchen this morning."

"I'm not sure I can even remember my ma's kitchen, much less her cooking." With his bowels still in turmoil the thought of eating anything repelled him.

He spotted Pete gathering up his bedroll, blanket, and gear, preparing to pack. Grabbing a tin of coffee, Jesse sought the companionship of his friend. "I can't eat a thing, Pete."

"Me, neither. Flux is runnin' rampant. And the medicine they give us isn't worth a damn."

"Let's see to the horses. Hopefully, they are feeling better than we are. As soon as I tell the others not to malinger, we can set out."

****

Jesse gently stroked the white blaze running along the bridge of Pretty's nose. "Good morning, Pretty Lady." The horse, in turn, eagerly nuzzled her trooper's hands and face.

"You're much too fond of that horse," teased Pete. "We gotta get you back to Miss Eliza fast."

They both measured their horses' feed before beginning the daily routine of preparing to ride. The horses always came first. They ate and then the troopers ate. They were groomed, watered, fed, and settled in for the night before the men even thought about doing the same. The horse was paramount, perhaps the difference between life and death.

As Jesse worked, he thought how some horse soldiers nearly hated the animals. To them they represented blisters, raw, chapped inner legs and thighs, and burning piles. Jesse had mostly worked through the sore legs. They were now strong and muscular, the skin on his thighs nearly as tough as his hands. He understood all too well about the piles, though, having suffered through his share. Most days he felt like he was riding with briers stuck in his trousers. The piles itched, burned, ached, even oozed blood. Hot baths were the common prescription for relief. Homeopathic drugs could be useful. Neither was close at hand near Wytheville. It did no good to bellyache. Though they were the bane of every cavalryman, no one ever died from the piles as far as he knew.

His practiced hands ran over Pretty's structure, feeling for any signs of injury or soreness. He checked the condition of both front hoofs and shoes. Jesse had always liked animals, whatever the variety: horses, mules, dogs, goats, pigs. It didn't matter. He would never blame Pretty for his discomfort.

"Would you choose bloody feet or piles?" he said to Pete. "If you had to choose one."

"What?"

"Bloody feet or piles? Remember Valley Forge? They said Washington's soldiers didn't have good boots. They wore out their shoes marching and wrapped rags around their feet. Then they were marching in crusty snow and ripped their feet apart."

"Golderned, Jesse, how do you know all that stuff?"

"Didn't you learn it in school, Pete?"

"Didn't pay much attention in school."

"Me, neither, but I learned to read and write well enough, and I always liked books, and stories— sometimes to my pa's aggravation. I've been thinkin' on our miseries and thought about those boys at Valley Forge. We've got good boots. Ridin' on a horse doesn't wear them out at all. But we got piles, which they didn't have, from bouncing on the back of these beauties all day." He was slowly working over Pretty's back, loins, and rear hoofs as he talked. He couldn't help but notice how her coat was thickening in the winter cold. "So, I was contemplating which was worse, bloody feet or piles?"

"We got piles, flux, and freezing feet as far as I can tell," groused Pete. "But returning to your insane question. It reminds me of the time that Daniel P. Murphy had me cornered in the alley between the broom manufactory and the wheelwright's shop. That sonofabitch gives me a choice. He says, 'You wanna get smashed in the groin or your ugly face?' He's holdin' this nasty club while I'm supposed to debate the issue."

"What happened?"

"I dove into him and beat him senseless with my bare fists before he could swing the club."

Jesse laughed. "You are a hard case, Strong."

"And to answer your question, General Washington, Sir." Pete gave Jesse a mock salute. "I will remain with my horse. I'll be damned if I wanna go marchin' through Ole Virginny."

Jesse was enjoying Pete's humor immensely. "Yeah, walkin's no good. I agree, but you'll march if I tell you to, Soldier."

"What those stripes did to you." Pete shook his head in feigned annoyance, a grin on his face. He gave his horse a final pat on the shoulder before setting out to walk back to the campsite with Jesse.

The wind was picking up. Both troopers instinctively wrapped their arms about their bodies, pulled their coats tighter, and scrunched their necks more deeply into the warmth of their collars.

"Jesse, I overheard an officer saying yesterday that we gotta be wary of frostbite. That don't sound good."

"It sure don't. I figure that's when your hands and feet get so cold you can't feel them at all."

"What happens then?"

"They hack them off."

"Jesus."

**The Lead Mines**
**Austinville, Virginia**
**Same Day**


The worst part was fording the frigid New River to get to the lead mine operations, their object of destruction. Two regiments were on the move, facing virtually no resistance. Two other regiments had been sent to Wytheville to raid the town, burn depots, and destroy the Confederate supplies.

The troopers in Jesse's squad hit the water almost simultaneously with an instantaneous cry of pain from the piercing cold. The river at the ford was fairly deep, up to the knees of the horses in spots. It was slow going, horses and riders careful of their footing. The freezing water splashed onto boots and trouser legs, soaking the occasional hem of a trailing greatcoat when a horse faltered or stumbled.

Jesse was content to cross slowly. Too much bravado on the part of a rider could find him in the river, washed away in the current, drowned. And there would be no surviving in this water. Before they had even reached the ford, word was spreading through the ranks to be on guard . . . *The river is wicked, icy, fast . . . Men have gone down . . . An officer washed away. No one able to grab him . . . Presumed dead.*

Pretty was a rugged, game mount. Jesse sometimes wondered who rode her before him. She had certainly learned her role, knew to follow those in the lead, knew to select her footing carefully, knew her objective was the opposite bank. He mused that he could fall asleep on her back, be slumped wounded or ill, and that she would know where to go, would not falter or throw him.

$$****$$

Once on the opposite bank, the lead companies pulled up. It was an opportunity to rest while waiting for the first of the artillery limbers to cross behind them, the wheels bumping and grinding over the treacherous river bottom. Jesse put the shivering cold out of his mind, maneuvering Pretty to a position where he could readily admire what was going on. He was endlessly fascinated by the designers and builders of the artillery caissons, wagons, and limbers. He knew wood, knew its strength and beauty. He was in awe of the power inherent in the entire operation, from the rugged artillery horses and the men who drove them, to the wood and iron structures themselves, and the fearsome firepower that they transported.

Once again, Stoneman's artillery executed a successful crossing. The line of march resumed, allowing the units guarding the artillery's rear to splash in behind them. And on it would continue. More troopers. Another artillery battery. More troopers. All headed towards Austinville.

$$****$$

The meager Confederate force detailed to protect the lead mines disappeared at the sight of the advancing Yankee cavalry, leaving the area unguarded save for a contingent of workmen. Charley gunned down one of them as the frightened man scrambled for the safety of the woods.

Jesse ordered the squad to hold up. They looked all too eager to bolt after the miners. "Let them go. We're as likely to get ambushed in there as to fell another one. They're gonna skedaddle to the winds. Let's follow orders. Destroy this place." He holstered his revolver and pulled out his rifle, which could serve as a club if need be. Pretty nickered and bobbed her head, as ready as the soldier who rode her.

The horsemen smashed what they could, set fire to what would burn, and stole livestock and anything of value that could be hauled away on their spare horses and wagons. Within two hours the mine offices, storehouses, stables, crushing machine, bellows, furnaces, sawmill, and gristmill were cleaned out and up in flames.

The artillery lashed out at the mines themselves. The massive guns collapsed and buried entrances, blew apart timber supports, wagons, carts, and tool sheds. They fired relentlessly into the earth itself, uncaring of man or beast that might still be inside.

Jesse stared at the spectacle. It was as close to Hell on Earth as he could imagine. Hundreds of horses and men. Soot-blackened faces. Choking, blistering smoke. Flames piercing the sky amid the violent cracking of disintegrating wood. Doomed structures outlined in blazing oranges and reds. Deranged shouting and cheers.

He felt oddly pleased. He was enjoying the warmth of the fire, its horrible beauty. It had been so easy. *No troopers lost . . . No opposition . . . Cowering civilian prisoners . . . Captured horses and livestock . . . So easy.*

Pretty was growing skittish around the fire. She balked a bit, backed up. Balked again. Jesse shifted in the saddle in an attempt to control her, thought of dismounting. As he turned his attention from the fire to the horse, he noticed the stains on his coat—the dried blood of the wagon guard. His mind leaped once again to that startled exploding face.

Blood and fire, fear and doubt, pain and destruction. That's all that seemed to exist in his world. No longer could he readily conjure up his ma's voice, Eliza's touch, Theo's boyish grin, or the warm feel of his coopering tools. He saw only that hideous face. He felt only the slap of Effie's hand, and the cold steel of his weapons. He heard only the sound of gunfire, and the moaning of men too frozen to continue soldiering.

His thoughts were interrupted by the crisp blaring of a bugle and the rapid fire of orders. Time to head out. The regiments from the lead mines and the regiments from Wytheville, the entirety of Stoneman's and Burbridge's commands, were to meet in Marion.

# CHAPTER 16

**Marion, Virginia**
**December 17, 1864**
**The First Day**


Burbridge's front regiment had easily pushed back the token cavalry force that Witcher had employed in his attempt to harass the Union advance.

*Where have the Rebs gone?* Jesse felt a strange mixture of euphoria and dread as he topped a rise to gaze down into a lush valley and its surrounding hills. It had been a fairly easy day. *No need to even fire my weapon.*

Stoneman had chosen the high ground overlooking the river as an obvious place to position the Union forces. The General knew the enemy was somewhere nearby. They had been alerted to Breckinridge's departure from Saltville, and Marion was the gateway to Saltville.

Jesse's platoon had dismounted, along with most of the company. Horses were being taken to the rear, guards posted to patrol the periphery.

Troopers were ordered to begin the tedious process of securing the position with light fortifications.

****

The initial gunshots whizzed over their heads. Jesse and Charley dove for the protection of a log they had been dragging from the woods. Their boots dug into the snow-crusted soil, which was quickly freezing after days of rain and snow showers. Their carbines proved difficult to control as they hurled themselves to the ground.

Jesse tried to ignore the pain in his shoulder, a result of the impact. He lay as low to the ground as possible, needing to see over the log but wanting its protection. "Where are they?" He was loading his rifle as he spoke.

Charley gestured with his own rifle, towards the distant trees, on the ground below them. The Rebel defenders appeared to be firing from below. "I'm thankful only one outta every 150 bullets finds its mark. Isn't that what they told us?"

"Somethin' like that."

"What do we do now, Corporal? Can't secure this place if we're hunkered down."

"Wait for orders." He obsessively checked his rifle, his cartridge box, his Colt. "Just be ready."

They were not ready for the thundering volley that ensued, the ungodly scream of the Confederate forces unexpectedly charging towards them. Before orders could filter down, Jesse barked one of his own to his squad within earshot. "Fire at will."

Jesse aimed, fired, aimed and fired again with the measured calm that comes of necessity. He was only vaguely aware that Charley was doing the same.

A trooper, someone he recognized but had no name for, seemed to explode before his eyes. *Cannon fire.* There was blood, gore. Much blood. It sprayed into the air, creating a fine red mist which filtered back on them and dotted the snow. Another man fell. *Elliot.* And then another. *His name was Elliot.*

The scene was chaotic. Uproar. Smoke. The firing of guns. Union officers trying frantically to form men into battle lines.

Pete appeared from nowhere, tumbling into the protective space between Charley and Jesse. "Son-of-a-bitch. I lost my rifle. God damn them all to Hell."

"Lay low," Jesse replied. "Use your revolver if you got it, or mine. You all right?" A cold trembling fear was beginning to engulf him, a primal fear that the act of firing was not dispelling. He sensed the same emotion in Pete.

"Elliot was . . . right beside me, Jesse. He just sort of . . ."

"I know. I saw it."

"Should we try to line up?"

"Here they come!"

It was like an apparition amidst the drifting gun smoke, the battle flag of the 10th Kentucky Mounted Rifles, that legendary Confederate regiment from his home state. Tough mountain boys. Biting into his lower lip, summoning his will to calm his trembling body, Jesse aimed at the flag bearer.

The Rebel boy's body reeled back in the same instant as the pain from his lip caused Jesse to gasp. The flag dropped, like a downed bird with a broken wing. Other soldiers clad in gray were advancing. Someone grabbed the flag, bearing it on.

There was screaming, cursing, running, chaos.

Soldiers were running towards Jesse, running past. Many of those running were wearing blue. He saw them both, blue and gray, and knew he must respond. He felt so cold, in both body and spirit—his resolve disintegrating. But he must respond. To the blood. To the gun fire. To the blood. To the fire.

*So cold! I . . . can't.*

It was the face of Satan that he saw next, charging straight at him. An avenging angel, intent on murder. He was coming, coming. Jesse fumbled with his rifle, cold fingers having no feeling at all. Each moment was surreal, as if he were watching a tableau, a play at the opera house.

*Respond. Do something!*

There was a momentary silence, that pause at the end of the play before the applause erupts. The slow, twisting fall. The final scene. The avenging angel was slain, a victim of Pete's revolver. Jesse heard a sickening thud as the man's body straddled the log that had been their defense. It jerked him back to reality.

"Retreat."

"Fall Back."

"Maintain order."

They heard the call again—voice and bugle—slicing through the mayhem. Stoneman's army was being ordered to retreat. Jesse shook his head, beating back the last remnants of his inability to act. He wanted to thank Pete, but there was no time. They scrambled to their feet, joining the mass of blue around them. Every man was running. Some paused to take a last shot. Some bore the wounded at the expense of their own safety. But all were in flight. To the horses. To safety. To the rear. Realizing in time that the 10$^{th}$ Kentucky, and whoever else was out there, had no intention of pursuing them.

****

The front regiments of the Confederate attack under the command of General Breckinridge had successfully eliminated Union resistance on the hills—Giltner's brigade having also joined in the rout.

"The high ground is ours," stated Breckinridge. "We now command the best defensive position on the field. But they will reorganize, Gentlemen, and hit us hard. Our element of surprise has passed. Suggestions?"

"Let us bolster our defenses with Major Page's battery, Sir. Position the artillery in such a way that it will slow the Union charge."

"See to it. Providence is, indeed, with us on this day. We will repel their charges, however many that may be."

"We could move forward under cover of darkness, have the men erect additional barricades to shore up our position," offered General Duke.

"You are correct, Basil. They cannot regain these heights before nightfall. It darkens early this time of year."

****

Burbridge's Union troops made three attempts that afternoon to regain the ground they had lost, three separate charges under fierce enemy fire.

At the onset of the first charge, Jesse had glanced down the battle lines forming around him. They were massing in columns, several companies wide, three or more ranks deep—a frontal assault. He was one small figure among thousands of dismounted horse soldiers, carbines in hand, flags aloft, ready to fight on foot. They had trained for such an assault, but few of them had been involved in more than a skirmish.

Sergeant Blackwood anchored one end of the line of their platoon, then five privates, Jesse in the center, five more privates, with another company corporal anchoring the opposite end

"Stay with me, boys," Jesse said to Pete on his right, Danny to his left, and anyone else within earshot. "Stay with me and the sergeant. We'll be all right. We'll take that Golderned hill right back from them."

He felt less confident than he sounded, felt more fear than he ever could remember. And shame.

He felt shame that he had practically frozen at the sight of the demonic Rebel who had come charging towards him. If Pete hadn't stood firm.

*How many are waiting for us now?* thought Jesse, immediately trying to drive the question from his mind. *Don't think on it. Not now. You gotta job to do. This day. Must guide the boys through what's to come. Must . . . Please, God, please, give me strength.*

The commands rang out, from officer to officer, echoing down the lines.

"Bri-*gade*!"

"Re-gi-*ment*!"

"Com-pa-*nee*!"

"For-'*ard*!"

"March!"

They moved shoulder to shoulder, not out of folly—for support. They marched close enough to be heard, close enough to warn, close enough to guide, close enough to encourage. They stood as close as brothers. They would fight as brothers, as they had ridden since the beginning.

The sergeants bellowed the orders passed down from the lieutenants and captains. "Close up, boys. Close up . . . Dress on the colors." And when they were near enough to inflict harm upon the men awaiting them—"Ready! Aim! Fire!"

\*\*\*\*

Jesse reclaimed his place in the line. They were advancing for a second time. Again, they could be ordered to break from formation, ordered to charge. They would then run in a crouch. Dodge. Fire. Seek cover. Crawl and claw a way forward. To run, dodge, and fire again. Hoping to draw nearer. Ever nearer. Yet dreading the proximity. Dreading to see the faces. Enemy faces so like their own.

His platoon had fared well in the first attempt across the field. They had tasted battle and were somehow intact. Each of them was now wearing the same determined scowl as they set out towards a well-entrenched enemy on higher ground.

Jesse would not look at the fallen as they advanced. He could not. Nothing mattered except his boys and one foot in front of the other. Reality was that step, his rifle in hand, instincts and training.

"It's those damn cannons," yelled Charley. "How we supposed to get through that?"

"Some o' our boys are flanking," Jesse assured him. "They'll take the guns out."

They were moving, a snake slowly winding through the grass. Pressing forward. Unsure. Towards the men on the hill. Until the snake shed its skin, roared like a lion, and charged—a blood-and-bones scythe sweeping through a field of horror.

Jesse felt the slamming of the guns, felt the reverberations in his cheeks, his lips. The big ten-pounders were hurling thunderous death, shaking the earth underfoot. When he stumbled, the guns roared their approval. When he strained to see, smoke blocked the sun. Sucking in a breath, he choked.

"This way," Jesse yelled. "To the left."

He saw Pete nod. Pete was close beside him, had been the entire way across the field.

It happened so fast, was sensed more than understood. The deep whine, the roar of the shell striking the ground just ahead. The teeth-rattling shock of it. The rifle arcing into the dark air, free of its owner's grasp.

"Pete?" Thrown to the ground, pommeled with dirt and debris, Jesse felt stabbing pain, the breath knocked out of him. He lay stunned, his breath coming back in gasps. He automatically glanced at his arms, his legs, his feet. Felt relief at being whole. Slowly, he began to move in the dirt. His chest hurt, and his heart pounded, but he needed to keep moving. "Pete?"

Jesse clambered to his knees, reached for his rifle, then struggled to stand. He felt off balance, confused. Furiously rubbing his face, he fought to breathe. Men were rushing past him. *Where are you going? Where's Pete? Where are my boys?* "Pete!" He yelled it again, wasted words, unheard in the deafening uproar.

Jesse found Pete sprawled on his back, eyes open—empty. His face was untouched. Blood oozed from the gore where his left arm should have been. Most of a leg was gone. His outstretched right arm lay peaceful in the brittle grass . . .

"No-o!" As he dropped beside Pete's mangled body, Jesse knew in his gut that Pete was dead. Yet he grabbed at his remaining arm and shook him.

"You can't just lie there, Pete. Come on. Wake up. We've got to get outta here. Pete . . ."

Jesse pressed his cheek near his friend's bluing lips. There was no breath. Accepting then what he already knew, he gently closed Pete's lifeless eyes.

He dragged Pete's body, dragged it, back through the fire and smoke, back through the debris of battle, back past the other dead, heedless through the hail of bullets, back to a safer, quiet place. Dry-eyed, retching, he dragged his brother until he could not.

"Corporal?" Someone took Jesse by the shoulders, helping him to his feet. "You've got to let him go . . . Come. We're regrouping."

Jesse stared at him. A strange officer from an unknown company. *Where's the 53rd? Where . . . ? Line up? Again?*

He stumbled after the officer. Obedient, dutiful. They thrust him into a line, his usual position, but with boys he did not know—boys who looked bedraggled, dazed, scared, lost. They were boys who badly needed his support, if support could come from the living dead man he felt himself to be.

Shouldering his rifle, he looked blearily down the line of weary troopers. Almost in a whisper, his throat raw, he managed to say, "Let's go, boys. Let's get 'em. Stay close. We'll be all right."

\*\*\*\*

Jesse looked up at the stars. It was a cold, clear December night. The Earth seemed no different. Stars shone the same as they had the night before. The moon still rose. But everything was different. Pete was dead.

Johnny Grubbs huddled beside him, their backs against the interior wooden walls of a covered bridge. Seventy-five troopers had been sent to hold it, at all costs, come morning and the resumption of battle.

"Do they really expect us to sleep, Corporal Jesse? Here? Like this?" Johnny was the youngest member of the platoon, no more than seventeen, having been permitted to enlist on the consent of his father. Jesse could sense the boy's fear, his barely repressed trembling.

"Try, Johnny. Lean on me. I don't think I can sleep a wink. I might as well help you."

"I'm sorry about Pete, Corporal. We all are. You and him were so . . . like brothers."

"Yeah . . . but it would hurt the same if it was you, Johnny, or Danny, any of you." Jesse pulled his greatcoat around his shoulders again and drew the blanket that they shared more tightly against their bodies. "Just try to sleep. Before you know it, it will be your turn to take the watch."

Grubbs soon began a fitful snore, his head lolling to one side, body propped on Jesse's upper arm, the darkness and cold enfolding them. All Jesse could hear was the distant, unmistakable sound of the Confederate soldiers fortifying their position, and the gentle lapping of gradually freezing water as it coursed past the bridge abutments to wherever it was going.

Jesse wanted desperately to sleep, to forget. But his tormented mind was seized by images, sounds, and feelings too raw to allow it.

# CHAPTER 17

**Marion, Virginia**
**December 18, 1864**
**The Second Day**


Sergeant Blackwood steadied his rifle on the ledge of the window opening in the bridge wall, preparing to fire outward as first light came to the Appalachian valley. The openings were above a man's height, designed to allow natural light to illuminate the bridge deck, but just perfect for a rifleman perched atop the catwalk built by the troopers the night before. "My God. Look, Jesse. Their breastworks are near on top o' our position."

Jesse had climbed up beside him. "I heard them working in the night. Can't sleep much when you're hearin' that." *Can't sleep much when other things are keeping you awake, either . . . Pete . . . Jesus, Pete.*

"What's the distance, you think? A hundred yards? Hundred fifty?"

"Bout that. Yeah."

Jesse continued chomping on a piece of hardtack, all that he had for breakfast. No fires, no coffee at the bridge. If they were to be effective, their presence must be a surprise.

"I'm goin' to make a final check with the men outside, Jesse. Firing will commence soon. You and Stu see to our men on the bridge. Looks like we get to open the ball this day."

It began at dawn. The soldiers at the bridge had one assignment, to harass the forward positions of the Confederate troops in preparation for the bulk of Burbridge's force to march when the fog had lifted. Jesse was thankful to be stationed on the structure with its built-in cover. He was thankful to be out of the hell which would rain down on the advancing columns of Union soldiers as they crossed the field.

As the day progressed they watched in awe as the Union regiments pushed back the Confederate 4th Kentucky Infantry, capturing the breastwork positions.

"Way to go, boys. Way to go!" Jesse was exultant, witnessing what could not be accomplished the day before in those three forays across the same ground.

He picked off another Southern boy on his own, someone who had stumbled too near the bridge while retreating from the field of battle. The enemy no longer had faces to Jesse. If they remained faceless, nameless, there was no guilt. Just revenge. Just a target.

"You got 'im, Corporal. Good shootin'."

"Thanks, Johnny," he said aloud, and then more quietly. "That one was for Pete."

He reloaded, taking aim again, searching for another gray coat. *Pete saved my life,* thought Jesse. *He saved my life, and then I . . .* He started to tremble at the realization. *Damn it.* He clenched his teeth and through sheer will steadied the rifle. *I'll kill them all. Every fucking one of them.*

****

General Breckinridge ordered his field commanders to counterattack. "Retake the breastworks; and, for God's sake, take out that damnable bridge."

"We'll move the 4th Kentucky to put pressure on the bridge, Sir. It will be done."

****

They came screaming as they always did, with that infernal Rebel yell. Jesse hated the sound of it, meant to scare the hell out of him and his comrades. "Ready, boys," he shouted in reply to the Rebels' advance. "Show your grit. Let 'er rip."

They seemed to have come from every direction, all at once. He saw from the flag that it was the 4th Kentucky. "Our own state," he muttered. "Fellas from our own state."

They were firing at will into the bridge. Finding targets. Felling troopers. An overwhelming attack. It made no sense to Jesse. Kentucky lads killing other Kentucky lads made no sense at all. He had ridden so far, to face across a battlefield, not Virginians, not

Carolinians, or Georgians, but Kentucky boys. For all he knew, they could be cousins of his, or cousins of Eliza.

Jesse grew more and more determined and agitated as the fight progressed. He was angry at what he considered misguided and wayward Kentuckians. They were inflicting such pain on his comrades, on their native state, on their own country. Pete was dead. So many were dead.

*For what?*

*Slavery?*

*Politics?*

Jesse aimed, fired, ducked for cover, reloaded and fired again. Each shot in answer to his own unbearable pain.

*Why did I ever say 'Go Left'?*

*Why?*

The intensity of Jesse's fight was not lost on his squad mates. They saw his carbine smoking, and when it failed to fire, they saw him grab his revolver.

\*\*\*\*

There was shouting all around him. Chaos. Running. Words too cruel to hear assailed his ears. Too cruel to bear.

"Fall back."

"Surrounded."

"Withdraw."

"Ve should go, Corporal. Der saying to go," remarked Krimmelbein. The big German crouched next to Jesse, ready to fire or ready to run.

Jesse was ready to fire. *Pete wouldn't bolt out of here,* he thought. *Pete would stand tall.*

"One more, Joe. One more." Jesse stepped out from the protection of the bridge wall, raising his revolver as he did so. He was about to take aim at a soldier splashing through the mud near the riverbank, but there was no time to pull the trigger.

The shot came from across the river, a 4th Kentucky infantryman had been eyeing Jesse. "I'll get you, you Yankee sumbitch. You're not taking down one more o' my boys."

Jesse felt a searing pain explode across his head. His body jerked back, slamming onto the bridge deck.

He tried to rise, but could not. He tried to speak, but could only groan. Warmth was spreading down his neck. *Blood . . . Oh, God.*

Joe bent over Jesse, gently lifting the corporal's head. "Mutter Gottes, Jesse, can you hear me?" Jesse blinked his eyes. Dizzy. Joe's face, blurring.

Joe tied a bandanna around Jesse's head, and it quickly soaked through with blood. "Ve must get outta here. I vill get you outta here." Jesse's head lolled to the side as he slipped into darkness.

Krimmelbein hoisted Jesse onto his back and began to stagger towards the Union's reforming lines. With Jesse's head resting against the German's shoulder, the blood soon stained them both. Joe knew he must hurry, a certain target for the advancing Rebs.

The other squad members, who had been nearby on the bridge, immediately knew Jesse had been hit. They scrambled to Joe's side, keeping pace with his stumbling gait, flanking to cover his retreat. Their presence buoyed Joe and he pushed onward. *Meine bruder,* he thought. *Lob sei Gott.*

∗∗∗∗

General Breckinridge relished the continual positive reports reaching his command. As the day progressed, their defensive position on the high ground seemed to be reaping benefits.

- *4th Kentucky now stationed near the covered bridge. Exacted heavy casualties on retreating Union forces. Union counterattack thwarted.*
- *Basil Duke: far right. After being pressed hard by columns of attacking Union soldiers; counterattacked Union line—routing it and forcing their withdrawal.*
- *Colonel Giltner: sending regiment to reinforce Duke.*
- *Duke and Wichter: combined forces on Union left flank. Inflicted significant damage to a Union colored regiment*
- *Burbridge withdrawing from the field. Breastworks held.*

"Almighty God." Breckinridge bowed his head in prayer. "I give thee thanks for

Thy guiding hand and providential grace in this most trying hour. I remain Thy humble servant . . ."

It was inexplicable. Outnumbered five to one, the fighting capabilities of his small force had created a reprieve for the salt works. *Only the hand of God in His beneficence . . .*

\*\*\*\*

General Stoneman was furious. Darkness had enveloped the battlefield. Reports were pouring in from field commanders and staff. He glared at General Burbridge, wondering if the man's bumbling would cost them Saltville for a second time. "Casualties?"

"Not yet definitive, Sir," reported a major from his staff. "Heavy in some regiments."

"Suggestions?"

"Prepare a counterattack." One of the commanders, fresh from the battlefield, had spoken up. Burbridge said nothing.

"How many more times do you suggest we storm their breastworks, General?"

"They are sorely outnumbered, Sir. They cannot hold indefinitely."

"And I cannot wait indefinitely," Stoneman growled. "Come tomorrow we must march on Saltville one way or another. We will lick Breckinridge, Gentlemen." He gazed grimly into the faces of his subordinates. "Now, see to the men. See to the wounded . . . Bury our dead."

\*\*\*\*

Sergeant Blackwood made his way slowly through the hospital tent. He felt like turning tail and running. God-awful odors. Weeping, moaning, muttering men. Passing the surgical tent had made him want to vomit. But he had come for Jesse. He had to know. The platoon had to know.

An orderly had taken him to Jesse's cot. "He ain't waked, sergeant. Them head wounds can be like that. Can't rightly tell about head wounds."

"Will he be all right, do you think? He has to be all right."

"Like I said, can't rightly tell. Might wake up tomorry. Might never."

"Never!" Blackwood dropped to his knees next to the cot, placing his hand on his corporal's shoulder. "Jesse, you rest now, but you wake up. You hear? You listen good. The boys . . . Me. We're all waitin' for you. Just, wake up. . ."

Jesse looked so deadly pale, so unaware.

The orderly had gone, but his words still poisoned the air for Blackwood. *Can't rightly tell about head wounds.* He felt like strangling the orderly, like strangling everybody in the goddamn army.

# CHAPTER 18

**Marion, Virginia**
**December 19, 1864**

**Pre-Dawn**
**Confederate Headquarters**

General Breckinridge gathered his field commanders for a final time. He felt ill, absolutely defeated. After the glorious way in which his outnumbered men had performed, repeatedly repulsing the Union advances, he would still be forced to abandon the field. It was unconscionable, unimaginable, but the only course to be taken.

"We are down to less than ten cartridges per man, Sir."

"Our stores in both Wytheville and Abingdon have been destroyed."

"Stoneman has confiscated our reserves of ammunition. There is little hope of resupply."

"We have so many killed or wounded . . ."

"Sir, I am not confident that we can hold back the Union force if they decide to attack."

The voices continued. Endless voices enumerating what he already feared. Pounding into his psyche. He must retreat from this field of battle before his army was completely destroyed. *Perhaps General Lee will forward an infantry brigade. Perhaps Lynchburg . . . We could head south.*

## Morning
## Union Headquarters

The Union generals were incredulous at the words they were hearing. "It is true, General Stoneman, they are gone. All of them, headed out."

The breastworks had been strangely quiet since daybreak. Nothing had alerted them to the stealthy departure of their enemy, and some time had passed before Union men were sent to prod the enemy position. It was now definitive.

"Gone," asserted Stoneman. "To where? Blocking our way to Saltville? Choosing new ground on which to make a stand? Do we know where the Southerners have gone, Captain?"

"It appears, Sir, that they are heading south. According to our scouts, they are headed away from Saltville."

"South!" Stoneman roared. "By God, Gentlemen, we may have the objective in our grasp." He slapped his gloves into the palm of his hand, the brisk winter cold suddenly less chilling. A strange warmth seemed to permeate his body. His eyes flashed.

"Gentlemen, our way to the saltworks lies open. It appears that we have weakened our adversary, and he is spent." Stoneman began to pace, exiting the HQ tent, his subordinates trailing behind him. Plans were rapidly forming in his mind. He surveyed what he could see of the camp, remembering all too well the carnage inflicted upon his army over the past two days. It fueled him.

"Generals Gillem, Burbridge, prepare your divisions to advance at first light tomorrow. Provide a sizable rear guard to protect the wounded and supply train. But, leave nothing to chance. We will defeat those bastards. Tomorrow . . . the day after."


## Midday
## Union Field Hospital


The dreams writhed in Jesse's outwardly composed body. Coming. Going. Someone placed an icy cloth upon his burning forehead, wiping it gently. They tried to lift his head and pour water into his mouth, but only succeeded in having it dribble over his chin.

Theo. His younger brother Theo was standing before him.

"You gonna shoot people, Jesse?"

"I don't know,Theo. Prob'ly not. There's no Rebs left in Kentucky."

"But you got a gun."

"Two, my carbine rifle and a revolver."

"Can I see 'em?"

"They're not with me, you goose. They're at the armory. I'll get 'em when I report for duty."

"When ya comin' back?"

"In a year. I signed up for a year."

"I wish I was goin'."

"Well, I don't." Jesse slapped his brother playfully on the top of his head. "You'd get yourself in all kinds of trouble. Besides, you gotta stay here and help care for Ma. With me gone, you're the eldest."

Jesse grabbed his brother by the shoulders and looked directly into his eyes. "Take care of her, Theo. It's on you now. She sometimes has trouble with Pa. You understand that, don't you?"

"I understand, Jesse."

"And, besides, you got to help Pa in the shop. You're not much of a cooper yet, but he still needs help."

# CHAPTER 19

**Saltville, Virginia**
**December 20, 1864**

**The Confederate Defense**

Colonel Preston gritted his teeth. The latest dispatch from his scouts had informed him that elements of the Union Army had arrived at the outskirts of Saltville, Gillem's 9th Tennessee Cavalry and its artillery battery. It was two o'clock in the afternoon.

"Is the entirety of Stoneman's army out there? Will they be?" He spoke to no one in particular. "Where is General Breckinridge? Where are my reinforcements? High command promised me reinforcements."

Preston was troubled. He had 400 reservists. Very old. Very young. Mostly untested. "There is nothing to do but fight," he muttered.

The Colonel turned his attention to his aide. "We'll take the initiative. Take the fight to them." He spoke with more confidence than he felt. "An attack.

We'll send a company down the ravine from the saltworks . . . Surprise them . . . It might buy us time until reinforcements arrive."


## Field Hospital

"Ma . . ."

"That's the first time he's spoken," declared a woman who had been attending Jesse and other wounded since the Marion engagement.

"Good." One of the army physicians glanced at her as he busily made his way through the tent. "Keep trying to bring him 'round. He needs to fully 'waken."

*"Ma, stop your crying. I can't have you crying."*

"My boy." She reached up to brush the stray hair from his forehead, to kiss him on the cheek. *"You look so handsome in your uniform."*

*"Ma-ah!"*

"Well, you do. Handsomer than your father even, when he was young."

*"Ma."*

"You make sure you come back to me, Jesse. Make sure."

*"Ma . . . Pete's dead . . . I killed Pete . . . Left . . . Go left.*

"Come home, Sweetheart."

*"Pete . . ."*

## Union Advance

Twilight, and General Stoneman was observing the action from the top of the hill. Colonel Stacy had taken the 13th Tennessee in a wide arc around the Confederate position in order to attack from an unexpected direction. From what the General could see in his field glasses, troopers were getting very close to the works with no opposition.

It had been a long afternoon, with a surprisingly stubborn group of reservists opposing his horsemen. The Confederate force had driven back successive assaults by both Generals Burbridge and Gillem.

Gillem's only success had been to break up an attempted surprise attack by Preston. The 8th Tennessee had sent the Rebs scampering back to their works down a ravine.

****

"Reinforcements," yelled a Confederate picket, jubilant with relief. "Reinforcements have arrived!"

The reservists ceased firing, staring instead into the gathering dusk at the advancing columns of horsemen, who came ever nearer. Until . . .

"They're not ours!"

"What?"

"No! No!"

"They're Yankees."

"Bastards."

"Gahdammit!"

Shots soon peppered the works and their defenses, aiming for the pickets on the line. Stacy's men were upon them, a thundering mass of blue devils on horseback, rifles blazing and swords flashing.

****

Stoneman saw it all. At the first sound of shooting from the 8th Tennessee he ordered a general advance of the remainder of his army. They came at the works from every direction. Within minutes the reservists were fleeing, abandoning the saltworks for the shelter of the town, the countryside, anywhere they could hide—if fortunate enough to escape.

The General sat taller in the saddle, a look of cruel satisfaction lighting his craggy features. After fourteen months the objective was finally in Union hands. In his hands.

# CHAPTER 20

**Saltville, Virginia**
**December 21, 1864**

**Field Hospital**

"Eliza . . . Liza." Jesse was stirring, waking up from a deep sleep. He felt groggy. His head throbbed. He just wanted to close his eyes and . . . *A woman.* Her voice was distinct. Then garbled. Her face was close, angular, ruddy, pale blue eyes. Then blurry, sliding away. *A dream?* He felt the pressure of her fingers supporting his chin, coaxing him to part his lips. *Who is? Where?*

"Come on. Just a sip."

"Liza?"

"That's not my name, Corporal, but I'm sure Eliza'd be wanting you to eat this." The woman gently guided a spoonful of broth to Jesse's mouth, relieved to see him finally rising to consciousness. He tasted warm liquid, too salty. Swallowing was rough. *My throat. So dry . . . Hurts.*

He lifted his arm, reaching to touch his head.

"Leave it be," the woman cautioned, lightly brushing his hand away. "You took a wound upside your ear . . . a bad scrape." Rattling the spoon in the bowl, she added, "You gotta eat for strength, to heal."

He reached up again, and she firmly lowered his arm. He couldn't resist. *So tired.*

Jesse licked his cracked lips, slowly turned his head. "Who are you? Where am I?"

"Shh," replied the woman. "Just open your mouth."

"A hospital tent," he muttered. Then, fully aware of the commotion around him, he stiffened, felt his heart leap in his chest— "Where's my boys? I gotta get outta here." He lifted his shoulder and pulled his elbow against his side, ready to heave himself up; but the room tilted and pain clawed his head. "Ahh," he moaned. A wave of nausea gripped his gut, and Jesse sank back onto the pillow.

The woman leaned over him, her fingers hard on his chest. "You're not going anywhere until you regain your strength. So, you first need to eat, drink, and rest. Now here—" The spoon rattled once again.

"What day is this?" he mumbled, blinking his eyes. Another spoonful slid into Jesse's mouth. He swallowed, beginning to savor it, slowly grateful. "Who took the field? In Marion? What happened in Marion?" More broth, warm, good. He tried to stay focused. "Where are my boys? The 53$^{rd}$?"

Suddenly stern, the woman's gaze held him. "Corporal, you were shot in the head and are lucky to be alive. Now, shush. And have some more."

He pushed her hand away. "My name's Corporal Jesse Cook, and don't shush me again. Has anyone been here to see me?"

With a dry laugh she said, "You know what, Corporal Jesse Cook, I think I liked you better when you were sleeping. Is that how you bark at Eliza? At least I can tell the doctor that you seem to have your faculties, for better or worse."

"Don't sass me, Ol' Woman. You can't keep me here."

She stood up, setting the bowl and spoon down. "So, I have to call the doctor now? Who is a *captain*, by the way, Cor-por-al."

Jesse shut his eyes, swallowed hard, heard her footsteps moving away. *What have I done? What would Ma say . . . and Liza? Forgot my manners . . . too long in the army. Is my brain?* His impulse was to touch the spot—the point of the throbbing. His breath came short, quick, and he felt his neck flushing, could feel his temperature rising.

The woman loomed up at the foot of the bed, a pinched ruddy smile on her face.

*Did she summon an officer?* Jesse dreaded the thought. Straining to raise his head, he blurted, "M'am . . . I am so sorry 'bout what I said. I didn't mean it. My Ma would faint dead away if she heard me talk that way to a woman." His head fell back on the pillow. "I'm sorry. I didn't know what I was doing . . . My head."

The dry laugh again. "I reckon that's true. But we'll get along better if you just open your mouth for the broth and keep it shut the rest of the time."

"Yes, 'M."

She sat by him again, taking up the bowl, the spoon, with a suppressed sigh. Jesse dutifully took whatever she offered. The broth was still too salty, but it was warm and soothed his throat, and he now allowed himself to sink into the act, accept nurturing, even relish it. He knew important matters hung restive just beyond his attention, and they wouldn't wait long; but for the moment he let the spoon and broth be his world. *And there's something about females . . . women . . . Liza. . .* His head drooped, too exhausted, in need of sleep.

Within minutes he jerked awake. He'd been in an uproar—faces, flashes, shouts, too vivid to be a dream, too alarming. The bridge. Krimmelbein. Falling. Danny, Charley, Johnny. Blood. Joe tying . . . He was remembering . . . all of it. His boys. Withdraw. Rebs coming . . . coming. Gunfire . . . An explosion . . . Pete . . . *Oh, God, were they all?*

His heart pounded, his breath growing ragged. He opened his eyes to find the soup woman on her feet, turning away, but halted as he lunged and grabbed the edge of her apron. "Do you know anything about my boys?" he pleaded. "Anything?"

"Corporal!" Prying loose his grip, she urged, "Please, don't' get yourself all riled up. I don't know anything about your boys, how they are, or where they are."

The noise had alerted an orderly, who called, "You need help?"

"No. We'll be all right."

The grief in Jesse's eyes had moved her, and so she sat by him again, a little apprehensive. *There's so much pain,* she thought.

Resting her hand on his hard lean arm was the only comfort she could offer. "I can tell you this much, Darlin'," she whispered. "Saltville fell last evening. We now control Saltville. General Stoneman was victorious. You boys are all victors today."

## Outside Saltville

The ragged remnants of Basil Duke's cavalry rested in the woods. Despondency hung in the air like a thick fog, suffocating them. At dawn they had attempted to reach the new Union defenses around the town and saltworks. A brief skirmish had proven the folly of the idea. The Union defenses were just too strong to breach.

"Flames were leaping in the air," proclaimed a Confederate reservist who had fled the saltworks the night before. "They was so bright it lighted our way out. Got me all the way to hereabouts. I tell you, twas like the sun was out."

One of the regulars glared at him in disgust. He had been disgusted when they had to abandon the field in Marion to the Yanks, and now this.

The reservist sensed the distain. "There was only 400 of us, mostly boys, and old men like me. We couldn't have done no better. Not up agin them. We held them back for hours." He paused, his voice growing softer, strained. "There was thousands of them. It was pure destruction, I tell you." Tears began to well in his eyes.

"You could hear their sledge hammers ringing agin the salt kettles and masonry kilns. Artillery shells rattlin' down the well casings." He paused, eyeing his detractor warily. "Soldiers was throwin' bags o' salt around like plunderin' Romans. Do you know about Romans, son? How they plundered and destroyed their enemies? The sheds, the stables, the offices. They was all in flames . . ." His voice cracked; his words now nearly inaudible. "We couldn't stop it. Couldn't."

# CHAPTER 21

**Marion/Saltville, VA**
**Army Field Hospital**
**December 23, 1864**

Stu reined in his horse, quickly dismounting and securing the bay to what remained of a farm fence near the medical field tents. Word had reached camp that the hospital units were moving out at sun-up. He had been granted permission to come by, to see how Jesse was, and report back.

"Everything in the army starts at dawn," he mused.

The place seethed with activity. One ambulance after another was lined up, ready to haul the wounded west to Catlettsburg, Kentucky, where they would be taken aboard river steamers bound for the military hospitals in Cincinnati, Covington, and Lexington. Ambulances were nothing more than covered wagons. Stu shuddered at the thought of the critically wounded being jostled overland, every rut and bump sending even more pain through their battered bodies.

*Best not think on it. Gotta find Jesse.* He quickly realized that the first in line to be evacuated were men borne on stretchers; so, he skirted around the orderlies and doctors attending to them, his eyes scanning the camp for the more ambulatory. Jesse should be among them. Their lieutenant had told the company noncoms that Jesse was out of immediate danger and out of bed. Now he'd find out for himself.

Groups of wounded soldiers were huddled around campfires, leaning against wagons, sitting on the bare ground or on crates and kegs. They were eerily quiet. The normal camp chatter of an army about to deploy was absent. Stu found Jesse seated on the ground, leaning against a tree, alone.

"Hey, Jesse." Stu sat down beside him. "Came to see how you are. Heard you were pulling out. We will, too. Tomorrow or next."

Jesse looked at him but did not speak.

*He looks . . . empty*, thought Stu. He tried again, "All the boys are okay, Jesse. They're wantin' to know about you. Can I tell them you'll be back?"

"I . . ." Jesse muttered something Stu could not even hear.

"What? What, Jesse?" Stu took the chance that his friend needed a little more than a kind word. He put his arm around Jesse's shoulder and drew him close. The December air was chilling. To his dismay Jesse seemed to collapse. His shoulders sagged. His head drooped. He seemed to be— weeping.

"Jesse, is it that bad? Does it hurt that bad?" Stu felt useless. "What can I do?"

"Nothing . . . Just go away."

"I'm not fucking going away," growled Stu. "What's wrong with you?"

Jesse lifted his head and pulled away from Stu. "I killed him."

"Who? What are you talking about? We all killed Rebs."

"No," Jesse fumed. "I killed *him*. I killed Pete."

"What?" Stu was confused. "He died in an artillery barrage. That was hardly—Any of us could've been hit."

"I told him to go left. Left, Pete. It's clear on the left, and, then . . ."

Stu bit his upper lip. Looking at Jesse's tortured face stunned him. *I don't know what to say to him.*

"You might not want to hear it. You, obviously, don't believe it, but, Jesse, Pete's death was not your fault." He got to his knees and gestured emphatically with his hands. "I don't know how to make you believe me. The rest of your squad is okay. You need to come back for them. Pete's gone. You cannot help him, but you can help the rest of the boys. They depend on you, Jesse. You haven't heard the way they talk, the way they look up to you. Everybody in the company respects you. From the top down, they think you're the best . . . You must have been one hell of a warrior on that bridge."

Jesse stared at him. Did not look away. *At least he's looking at me,* thought Stu. *Maybe he's listening.*

"Your boys are taking care of Pretty for you," Stu continued. "They asked me to tell you. When we ride out, Pretty will be with us, waiting for you when you come back."

"I failed him, Stu. I led Pete wrong . . . *Said Go Left.*"

"You didn't fail him, Jesse. Pete would be the first one to tell you that." He took Jesse by the arm and helped him stand up. "Can we find a warmer place to wait for your ride, Bub?" he asked.

Jesse shrugged. "It is Golderned cold."

"Jesse," Stu said. "I need your help. One of my boys is in one of the front ambulances. You remember Jim? The fellow with the lisp?"

"Sure," Jesse replied.

"Jim is frostbit, real bad." Stu swallowed hard. "He's afraid he's going to lose his leg. At least his foot. Jesse, he's not comin' back and he's scared. He's really scared. He needs me, but I can't be there. I'm askin' you. Dependin' on you to help him however you can."

Jesse looked tortured. *I can't help*, he thought. *It's no good.*

"Don't tell me you can't," said Stu, as if he were reading Jesse's thoughts. "Even in a hospital ward, you're still a corporal from the 53$^{rd}$, and Jim is one of our boys."

"Have you completed the lecture?" Jesse asked, and for the first time Stu thought he saw a spark of his friend's old spunk. "You're as much of a hard case as Strong was. Don't give me a moment's peace. Always goin' on about somethin'. Ever free with your opinions." Jesse drew his coat tighter, crossing his arms across his chest. "Frostbite's deadly. I know. Heard a doctor growling about it in the tent. The trouble is they're not too good at treatin' it." He sighed, "Except for whackin' off bits and pieces of you." He pressed Stu's arm. "I'll check on him. I don't know what the hell I'll say, but I'll check on him for you."

"Just havin' you there, Jesse, will help. Now, I gotta get back. And it looks like they're beckonin' for you." He gestured towards an orderly who was helping men get seated in an open wagon.

"Looks like I'm going in style," muttered Jesse. "Wish they'd let me ride, but they won't."

"You'd fall off the damned horse."

Jesse smiled for the first time. "Not off of Pretty. We're a good team."

Stu patted his friend's shoulder. "Get well, Chum. We need you back."

As he turned away, Jesse called after him. "Stu, tell the boys I'll . . . I'll try. Tell them that."

"Come along, Corporal," said a medic. "Let me give you a hand up."

"Thanks."

"And here's another blanket. Yer gonna need it."

Jesse called frantically after his departing comrade, "Stu, tell the boys."

Suddenly Stu was running back towards the wagon, a letter held high in his hand. "Jesse, I almost forgot. This is for you. It's from Eliza. Yeah, from Eliza. You're going home to your sweetheart."

Jesse held the letter reverently. It had been so long since any mail had reached him.

"What was it you wanted me to tell the boys, Jesse?"

Jesse swallowed, looking squarely at him. "Tell them I'll be back."

Stu grabbed his friend's hand in a warm handshake. "I will. Gladly."

"Move 'em out!"

"I'll see ya, Jesse," said Stu. "Good Christmas to you."

"Thank you. For everything."

"Gee! Ha!" The teamsters prodded their lead horses. Leather and wood groaned, and wagons creaked forward.

Unheard amid the commotion, Stu whispered fervently, "I hope to God I see you again."

# PART FOUR

# THE BETTER MAN

# CHAPTER 22

## Christmas Day
## 1864

"He won't come back the same, Henry." Riley Cook inhaled the aromatic smoke of the cigar his brother had offered as a Christmas respite. "He's seen things. Tasted things. He'll be changed."

"No doubt. He was already changing 'fore he left."

"I don't relish it. A man looks forward to his sons' coming of age, but . . ."

Henry glanced at his own eldest son who was romping across the parlor, "It's a long ways off for me. Jimmy being all of six." He studied his brother. "What exactly is troubling you, Riley? That Jesse'll want to settle down with Eliza, start his own family? He's old enough."

"Nah." Riley stared at the crackling wood in the fireplace. "Don't mind that." He seemed to hesitate, then turned from the fire to face Henry. "Jesse may prove to be a better cooper than I am. Be better at business."

"Shouldn't you take pride in that? You taught him the trade, after all."

"It's just Jesse's way. He has these big ideas. Wants to expand. Hire men. Start a *manufactory* . . . But he'll learn."

"He's young, Riley. That's what he's supposed to do. Want more. Dream." Henry flicked cigar ashes into the fire. "Aren't you planning on taking him into the business?"

"He'll work for me. That won't change."

Henry pointed his cigar at Riley's chest. "Work *with* you, Riley. Change the way you think. You won't lose him and you won't regret it later if you change the way you think. Make Jesse your partner."

"Partner? At twenty?" Riley groused. "It took me a Golderned long time to get my own shop."

"And I would assume that one of the driving factors in getting your own shop was that your family would have it easier than you," countered Henry. "J.R. Cook & Son. Sound good?"

"I, er, don't know. What's wrong with Cook's Cooperage? Says it all. I have four sons, as you know." He chomped on the end of his cigar—a bit piqued.

"But Jesse's the eldest . . . Ask his opinion."

"He'll want Cook & Cook, with him being the first Cook because of the alphabet or some such nonsense. You don't know Jesse."

"I do know Jesse," growled Henry, "and what you put him through. He's earned his right to a say."

Riley glared at him, but Henry just gave a slight, sure smile.

"Jesse's going to come back a man, Riley. Not the boy who left us. If there's one thing that matures a man, it's goin' to war. You'd better come to terms with it."

"*If* he comes back." Riley lowered his voice, spotting Henry's wife Sarah swooping into the room.

"Dinner is served," she smiled. "Come along, all of you. The Christmas feast awaits." Her outstretched arms beckoned the four little Cook cousins who had been playing on the parlor floor. She looked towards her husband and brother-in-law, "Gentlemen?"

"Have you heard the news coming out of Virginia?" Riley murmured apprehensively.

"Yes," replied Henry, snuffing out his cigar. "Don't think on it, Riley. The reports are preliminary. Haven't read anything about the 53rd." He patted his brother on the shoulder. "Let's try to enjoy ourselves at dinner. Talk about anything but this."

****

They had been traveling up the valley for two days, heading for a pass through the mountains, heading towards Catlettsburg in Kentucky, where they would board a steamboat. With a Kentucky contingent mounting guard, there had been no incidents.

This section of Virginia was defeated, scarcely a Reb to be seen as far as Jesse could tell. Once beautiful country, now war torn and weary. It depressed him. He was tired of watching people suffer. Tired of the cold. Tired of feeling weak and dizzy, his head aching. Always aching. And it was Christmas.

They stopped for the night at a town that seemed almost welcoming. He knew not where they were, nor did he care. It would be a night of relative warmth, in a building, finally.

*Like Bethlehem,* Jesse mused. He was sitting on the floor of a hallway, leaning against a paneled wall, his bedroll by his side. He fingered the polished wood. *Nice work. Master carpenters.*

Two other soldiers rested nearby, close enough to touch. One had a heavily bandaged arm in a sling. About the other fellow Jesse could not tell. There was no sign of a wound. The boy never spoke, just shook uncontrollably from time to time. Having ridden with him the past two days, Jesse wondered if the fellow was somehow wounded inside, in his mind. The nurse, after all, had mentioned the fact that Jesse had his faculties. *Could just be a coward, the lad with the shakes, I suppose. But...*

"Corporal, have some Christmas cheer." The medic with whom Jesse had grown friendly offered to pour him a dram of rum.

"Tom, where did you get this?" Jesse smiled briefly, knocking the spirits down immediately. The warmth of it seemed to spread through his entire body.

"Do you doubt that the U.S. Army takes care of its own?" Tom offered drinks to the other troopers in his good-natured manner, then returned his attention to Jesse. "What about him, Corporal?" he asked, gesturing to the mute. "Should I?"

"Give it to me, Tom. I'll see if he wants it . . . Oh, and a refill?" He held out his cup.

"Don't get wallpapered, Corporal."

"I wish."

"I still can't drink with my left hand," said the boy with the arm sling. "Half the rum's down my jacket."

"What a waste," replied Jesse as he shifted his position some so that he could face the silent one.

"Here, chum. This'll warm you. Sweet, sweet rum."

The boy simply stared at him. Jesse tried again, this time passing the cup nearer the soldier's nose, tempting his senses. Startled, the boy jerked back, then lashed out, knocking aside his hand. Rum flew, making dark stains on Jesse's jacket and trousers.

"Tarnation!" Jesse yelled. "What's wrong with you, Private?" He wiped his hand on his sleeve and gulped what little was left in the cup himself.

"He's tetched in the head," said the boy with the arm sling. "A Nancy coward, I'd say."

Jesse leaned back against the wall and sighed. "Maybe. Maybe not." His own struggle with courage was too fresh in his mind to accuse anyone else.

"Yeller as my mama's dress," continued the boy. "Oughta shoot him."

Jesse scowled. "I think enough of us have been shot, Private. Shut your mouth."

Several yards down the hallway an older fellow glanced over. "You have any idea what this place used to be, Corporal? It's a fine building. Seen you admiring it earlier."

Jesse was taken aback at first, not realizing the man was even speaking to him. *Probably wanting to change the conversation,* he thought.

"Guild Hall," he replied. "I saw the insignia in the front room where we came in. Coopers. Mechanics. Smithies. All meet in here."

"Ah. I guess that explains the good carpentry."

"It does. Do you work with wood yourself?"

"Only what a farmer needs do. Don't go to town much . . . You?"

"Cooper," replied Jesse. "My entire family are coopers, 'cept for one renegade uncle who decided to manufacture brooms."

"I tried makin' my own barrel once," said the man. "Couldn't do it. Leaked like a sieve. Staves wouldn't bend. Hoops fell off. Ungodly mess."

Jesse chuckled, "That's why we build guild halls, to safeguard the secrets."

They sat in silence for a while, until the man spoke again. "I don't rightly take that boy for a coward."

*So much for a change in conversation.*

The man continued. "What we seen out there—and what we couldn't do."

"Yeah," whispered Jesse in reply.

Silence settled over the group once again. A soft moan, a cough, or a whispered comment could be heard now and then, but nothing more. The men embraced their own thoughts for what little solace they offered, until the strain of a Christmas tune came filtering down the hallway. Somewhere out of sight someone had begun playing a harmonica. The haunting melodies of "Hark the Herald Angels Sing" and "O, Come, All Ye Faithful" wrapped around them. The popular old carols settled over the soldiers like a soft mantle.

Jesse slumped to the floor, resting the good side of his head on the bedroll. *Christmas,* he thought. *Is it really Christmas when you're in a place like this? Are they celebrating at home? With me and Uncle Frank both off to war? Is Henry hosting the entire family again? Maybe even Uncle Val Gentry? Last year . . . The first time they included me in the cigar ritual. Reckoned I was old enough . . . Pa's handmade wooden toys for Willie and Jimmy . . . I helped carve those . . . Damned miniature wagon wheels. Coaxin' them from that ornery piece 'o pine. And Theo. He's too old for playthings now . . . Maybe Pa made him his own adze handle, embellished with initials. Like he did for me once . . . What a pleasure to hold that beauty in my hands . . . Eliza.*

The sound of sobbing pierced his reverie. The mute boy was weeping. Jesse sat up, carefully stretched his back, and glanced at the boy. He was moving his lips, but his voice was still as silent as the tears coursing down his face.

"You gonna talk, boy?" mocked the soldier with the injured arm.

Shooting a warning glare at the mouthy fellow, Jesse scooted closer to the distraught boy. He slid his arm around the private's shoulders. "You're safe, bub," he said.

The boy mumbled incoherently.

"What?" asked Jesse, leaning closer in an attempt to hear.

"Christmas . . . my pa . . . sing."

"Your pa used to sing at Christmas?" replied Jesse. "That musta been real nice. My family likes to sing, too." He pulled the boy tighter around the shoulders. "Just imagine you're back there. We'll all be home soon."

"Sing." The boy was growing agitated. "Sing," he said even louder.

"Okay. Okay. I'll sing . . . I'll sing for your father.

*"Si..i..lent Night,*
*Ho..o..ly Night.*
*All is calm.*
*All is bright . . ."*

Jesse's baritone rang out bravely, grateful for other voices that soon joined in. His own voice choking with emotion, he relied on the soothing lyrics of the familiar hymn to calm the private as well as his own ailing soul.

# CHAPTER 23

## On the Ohio

A dense shadow lay over his face. What light shone from lanterns within played with the boat's window frames, decking, doors, and railings, setting a ghostly scene. Jesse walked the deck between the softly glowing spots, letting the darkness envelop him, feeling a part of it, as dim and deep as the night.

His wound was healing, though his head still pained him. Dizziness and nausea lingered. But at least he was on his feet, off the cot, away from the putrid odors and blood-soaked bandages, from the amputees like Stu's frightened young Jim, from the boys who knew they were dying.

Momentarily lightheaded, Jesse clung to the rail. His thoughts drifted back to summers past, sitting on the riverbank, watching the steamers plow majestically towards Louisville, St. Louis, St. Paul. He had yearned to climb aboard such vessels, pushing off for ports only half-imagined. He of course had never pictured making a river journey of this kind, as a patient on a steamboat converted to a floating Union Army hospital. Gilt and glamour, dreams and adventure reduced to agony, fear, and sorrow.

He pulled his coat more tightly about him. The winter's cold never let up, gave no mercy. Ice was forming on the river. As it scraped the hull, he wondered about the safety of that but knew to stop could mean becoming completely iced in. So, the captain urged the boat cautiously, determinedly forward. It needed to reach Cincinnati and Covington, sites of the military hospitals and home. Jesse's coat was roomier than before, as was his uniform; for the one wound had taken its toll on his entire body. Between the nausea and the hospital smells, he hadn't much of an appetite.

They had eyes like his, the dead. He always noticed their eyes. Remembered them, Reb or comrade, for their eyes were the same. Unfocused, vacant, staring. And they were eyes just like his. Blue. Brown. Grey. It didn't matter. They were eyes of the young with no future.

Slow footsteps scattered his thoughts.

"Is that you, Corporal? I seen you leavin'. Thought I might do it myself."

Jesse recognized the voice. The man's face was in the shadows. It was Tom, the medic from his regiment, a slight fellow who managed to exude both confidence and strength, while looking capable of neither. Jesse had no idea how the medic could stand his job, his sleeves always thick with blood and vomit.

"Heard tell we're two days out," Tom continued. "Wanna cigar? Might do you good. Settle your stomach." Jesse accepted the offer. Allowed Tom to light it. "Hell of a thing, going home, Corporal. Expect I'll see my folks. And you?"

Jesse shrugged. "I can't imagine that. Don't even know if I want to."

"I unnerstand. Me, too. Hard to know what to say to folks who haven't . . ."

"Do you ever feel like two separate people?" interrupted Jesse. "I swear a part of me is back there lying in Virginia, dead, and buried with my pard Pete." He stared unseeing into the river. "Sometimes . . . Well, all the time, I wonder why I wasn't killed. Shoulda been." He took a long puff on the cigar. "Prime Kentucky tobacco. Pete woulda liked this."

"I know exactly what you mean, Corporal. How do we talk about the weather, politics, what's for dinner, everyday things . . . knowin' what we know? Seein' what we seen?"

"Maybe the army is our family now, Tom." He gestured towards the South. "My platoon is out there somewhere, on the march, tryin' not to freeze to death. I should be with them. Not here."

"Mebbe so. Mebbe not." The medic touched Jesse's arm. "Corporal, you best get back inside. I don't wanna have to tend to you again. You're not the world's best patient." He put his arm around Jesse's waist, ready to support him if necessary. "I figure you want to go back to the regiment. They'll send you if you just mend a little more."

Jesse chuckled at the bad patient remark. It felt cleansing, for he hadn't laughed much of late. Flicking the ash from the cigar into the river, he willingly draped his arm over Tom's shoulders.

# CHAPTER 24

**Covington, Kentucky**
**January 4, 1865**

The anteroom in the military hospital was uninviting, bare except for the desk of a sullen clerk enduring his assignment. Apprehensive, Riley had hurried to inquire about Jesse after being startled to see his son's name in the morning newspaper, listed among the wounded brought back from Virginia by the steamer *Telegraph*. He knew nothing else—the nature of Jesse's wounds, their extent, their effect on him.

However, on arriving at the hospital, Riley had been given reason for a sigh of relief. Hoping only to catch a glimpse of Jesse, he'd been told to wait—his son would be released within the hour. Not knowing what to do during that interminable span, Riley shuffled back and forth, hands in his coat pockets, snapping his fingers, and chewing on a matchstick, while time stood still.

A door opened. A man and woman—no one Riley knew—were coming out, obviously distraught. Beyond the couple, he took in a corridor. A nurse was pushing a cart piled high with linens and other supplies. A priest, in the long flowing cassock of the Roman Catholic faith, stopped to speak with her. His crucifix, strung boldly about his neck, lay pronounced against the black fabric. The nurse appeared to be giving him directions. Riley looked away, knowing the meaning of a priest's visit. What the Papists called Last Rites. With a deep self-reassuring sigh, Riley nodded to himself—no, not Jesse.

Just before the door slammed shut, Riley caught sight of Jesse at the near end of the corridor. He leapt for the door. "Halt!" barked the clerk, his finger tapping the pistol resting on the desk. "No goin' in there."

Riley's hand fell from the door just as Jesse thrust it open and stepped out—Jesse, sickly pale and lost in his rumpled greatcoat, with a stark white bandage covering the side of his head and much of his hair. A husky murmur—

"Pa!"

"Son!" *Oh, Lord. That bandage. A head wound.*

Moving past him and half turning, Jesse let his haversack and bedroll slide with a *thump!* to the floor. Under his open coat the butt of a revolver showed. *A fighter . . . a killer. No, a fighter. My son.* Riley flexed his right hand, ready to take Jesse's, which seemed to hover half way between them, uncertain.

"Welcome home, Corporal." He gripped his son's hand in both of his. Rough, hard, thin.

The urge to lock arms in an embrace, felt and rejected by both, passed. Jesse thought, *Corporal— Why'd he call me that? A joke? Or not?* His gaze met Riley's briefly, flicked away, flicked back, swept the room, while he slipped his fingers free. "Tarnation, Pa."

Plunging his hand into his coat pocket, Riley growled, "Tarnation, Jesse."

The two men stood then, frozen for a moment like figures in a wax-works, Riley looking for a sign, a clue, in Jesse's ever-startling pale gray eyes. A question tried to form on Riley's lips, but Jesse spoke first. "Let's move out."

"You're free to go?"

"Yep. Home . . . for a while."

"Free t' go. Tarnation." With a bewildered but deeply satisfied grin, Riley gestured towards the front door. "Your Ma will jump out of her skin." He bent to retrieve the gear.

"Let me, Pa."

Riley shook his head. "You oughta take advantage of service while you can. This is the best it'll get."

"Right, Cap'n." Jesse pulled a soft cap from his coat and gently squared it over the bandage.

"No, hold it," Riley muttered, drawing off his heavy scarf and stepping to Jesse, quickly covering his neck and ears. "Now *that's* the best."

A muffled grunt was the answer.

Shoulder to shoulder, father and son strode out to engage the biting January air.

\*\*\*\*

Catherine had wanted to go with Riley. From the moment he had showed her Jesse's name on the list of the wounded, she had vacillated between relief and terror.

Jesse hadn't been killed. Praise be to God! But he was hurt . . . How badly? Was he whole? Lame? Blinded? Her mind kept scrambling, conjuring up horrid pictures of her dark-haired boy forever changed. Her precious firstborn son.

She longed to go to Jesse's side, to see for herself. But she and Riley couldn't both go. There was the baby to care for, the other youngsters, and the shop. She would go tomorrow. Surely Riley would allow her that, to go tomorrow, after he told her what to expect—whatever that might be.

*What is taking you so long?* she thought. *Oh, Jesse . . . I must know.*

She would go to him. She could not contain herself, could not deny herself a moment longer. She would stoke the fire in the stove and call Theo in to tend the younger ones. Josiah, the hired man, could see to the shop until Riley returned. She would tell him.

"Ma!" Theo burst into the kitchen, shocking her from her trance. "Ma, Jesse's here! Jesse's come with Pa . . . I swear it, Ma. I seen them!"

Catherine scooped the infant, Willie, into her arms, pulling her shawl over him, and ran towards the shop. They arrived nearly simultaneously. She from the rear; Jesse and Riley from the alley. She thrust Willie into the arms of a startled Josiah and nearly flew across the rough planks, somehow avoiding benches, tables, casks, and tools.

She enfolded Jesse gently in her arms, not wanting to cause him further pain. Catherine stood on tiptoe to kiss his bristly cheek. She then stepped back, and cautiously unwound the scarf and let it drop. Taking both of his hands in her own, she led him to a stool and whispered, "Sit."

Now she could fully see and hold him properly. Ever so tenderly, Catherine stroked the uncut swath of the thick dark hair she knew so well. She lightly kissed it, and then stretched to cradle Jesse against her breast. "Jesse . . . Oh, my boy."

Weeping silently, she felt her son's tensed and battered body begin to tremble against her own.

# CHAPTER 25

**Mid-January
1865**

    Jesse felt like he had been sleeping forever. But what a relief it had been to merely sleep: in a bed, in his father's house; away from the smells, sights, and sounds of a hospital; away from the cold, dirt, and damp of army camps; away from the jarring ride of a wagon.

    He had been home about a week by his reckoning, doing mostly *nothing.* Just resting and getting "fattened up," as his ma liked to say. It was comforting but peculiar. He had been welcomed warmly, of course. Neighbors and relatives had come and gone. People dropped off food. But no one treated him as they did before. He felt like a sideshow attraction:

> *Come see the amazing boy*
> *Who got shot in the head*
> *And lived to tell about it.*
> *A PHENOMENON!*
> *He's got half a head of hair.*
> *A tad crazy he is,*
> *But don't let him scare you.*

"Yeah, don't let him scare you," he muttered. He swung his feet onto the floor and got up. "Today it stops."

Dressing quickly in the cold air of the bed chamber he bounded downstairs to the kitchen. His mother was there, as usual. "Jesse, you should be resting. I'll bring you something . . ."

"No, you won't." He grabbed a hunk of bread, slathered some butter on it and headed for the door. "I'm going to the shop." He stopped short, regretting his abruptness. "I'm okay, Ma. I need to work, that's all . . . I appreciate everything you do."

Pulling on an old work coat, he kissed her on top of her head. "I would like a cup of your coffee, though," he said. "Anytime you get the chance. I'll be with Pa."

Riley didn't act particularly surprised to see his son, which heartened Jesse. "I had a notion you'd want to get back to work," he said.

Jesse grabbed his work gloves and tool belt. "What can I do?"

"Whatever suits you," replied Riley.

"Finishing work maybe. I don't feel up to splittin' wood."

"Pull up a stool."

The hired man glanced over at the two of them, father and son. "Want me to deliver the Schulz order?"

"That'd be good," said Riley.

Jesse watched the man exit towards the modest stable where they kept their dray horse and wagon. "Guess I scared him off . . . Feel like a sideshow these days."

"Nah, Josiah's seen it all. Good bit older than I am . . . Asked him to leave whenever you showed up."

"Why?"

"Hopin' you'll talk to me, and you probably wouldn't in front of him. Not knowin' him and all."

"What am I supposed to talk about?"

"What you never say in front of the women, the young'uns."

"Maybe there isn't anything to say."

"And maybe there is."

Jesse busied himself, expertly making needed adjustments for a perfectly fitting barrel lid. When finished with that task, he yanked his stool to another job. He could sense his father's eyes following his every move. Did not look at him. "What?" he finally said.

"It's good to have you here again . . . workin' side-by-side . . . I told Henry at Christmas you were going to be a better cooper someday than I ever hoped to be."

"What!" Jesse laid down the chisel he held and stared at his father. "You actually said that?"

"I've known it for a couple of years. As a young lad, you showed good work sense early."

"Dang . . . Well, thanks, Pa. Though I probably lost my touch over these past months. Out of practice."

"Um."

Jesse resumed his chiseling. "What did Uncle Henry say to that comment?"

"Said I should make you a partner in the business."

Jesse stopped what he was doing and looked at his father, mouth agape. "Partner?"

"Not right away, of course. You're still a might young, and I'm not quite ready, but soon enough—after you've wed and settled into a family of your own . . . When we see how this war changes things."

"Partner? Tarnation . . . Fifty-fifty?"

"Well, maybe sixty-forty."

Jesse grinned, "I accept, before you say seventy-thirty." He thrust out his hand to shake his father's. "Tarnation. I'll be . . . Just, tarnation." He got up from the stool and began to walk around the shop, studying everything as if interested in purchasing the place. He looked up, down, from the alley front back towards the door to their family rooms. Mentally he scanned the side yard, storage area, and stable—just out of sight.

"Sometimes when I couldn't sleep, I'd think of this place. What I, er, we could do to expand. Grow the business," he said.

"I've no doubt you did," replied Riley.

Jesse laid his hand on the smooth varnished handle of his adze, the one his father had made for him in his 17th year, not long after Riley's release from prison. The gesture was not lost on his father.

Jesse was still facing the tool storage when he began to speak. "I met a young cooper in Virginia—not much older than Theo—about the age I was when you went to Joliet. We were raiding the town where he lived. Looting. Wrecking anything of value. I shoulda destroyed, maybe even burned, that shop. But . . . I didn't. I couldn't. Not when I saw his face. Sensed his fear—of me, Pa—of me. Not when I remembered."

Riley said nothing.

"You were right, Pa. There's nothing glorious about any of it . . . Not the shooting . . . Not your churning gut . . . Not chums dying before your eyes." Jesse attacked a small workbench, upending it in anger, sending items banging and crashing around the shop. "Nothing glorious at all."

He slumped to the floor. "Sometimes I wished I had died, Pa." He touched his scarred head. "Instead of this."

Riley came over and sat down beside his son.

"I couldn't save Pete." He looked at his father with tears in his eyes. "I led him wrong, Pa. Through the smoke. The wrong way. I said 'left' . . . And then." Jesse shut his eyes tightly, as if that action could blur the memory. But other thoughts crowded in. "And Ma's cousins. My cousins . . . I met them. Just like she said I might. I can't tell her I failed those people. They wouldn't listen to me, Pa. That girl wouldn't leave with us . . . under our protection. Her name was Effie . . . probably dead, by now. And her old grandfather . . . I wonder if Ma knew him."

Riley reached out, grasping Jesse by the shoulder. "Look at me, Son." Jesse did, and the pain in his son's eyes gripped Riley hard.

"I'm not much on giving advice, Jesse. Not much of an example. But this I know. I know a good man when I see one. And I'm lookin' at one . . . You may think you failed in some way, but I know better. You did what you could. You did what you had to do. You can't ask more of a man than that . . . No one can ask more."

Jesse did not reply. Riley removed his hand but did not change his sitting position. Noticing Catherine, coffee in hand, at the back of the shop, he motioned her away.

"When I was a young man, 'bout your age, startin' off as a cooper in Cincinnati . . . The city was growing like blazes. Rough. Wild. Sometimes lawless. There was a lot of unrest. Stinking slums. Too many newly come Irish worked the waterfront, elbowing free coloreds and runaway slaves for jobs. Fights, even organized riots . . . Thugs and boys tight on liquor just took advantage of the situation. They wrote it up in Eastern newspapers it was so bad. Think there was as many in jail as out of it. I was one of 'em . . . off and on. Illinois was not my first arrest, Son."

"Why are you telling me this now?" Jesse growled. "Though I always suspected as much."

Riley hesitated, then said slowly, "I just thought you should know I've seen my share of violence. Felt my own gut turn. Feared for my life— that of other fellas. . . Not that anything I've been through can equal what you've faced."

"Have you ever killed a man?" asked Jesse with a sharp intake of breath.

"Not sure . . . I could have. Certainly left them for dead. Intention's the same."

"Jesus Christ, Pa!" Jesse didn't know whether to stay or run. Part of him was recoiling in horror at his father's admission. Another part saw a boy not unlike himself, so afraid and backed into a corner that he'd do anything to survive.

"You did your duty, Son. Answered the call of your country. You fought and killed for a greater good . . . I have no excuse for what I did. Nothin' noble about it. Or me."

Riley pulled himself up from the floor using the rim of a barrel to aid his ever-aging knees. He limped to where the cups of coffee sat waiting. Picking one up he looked full at his son, meeting Jesse's eyes. "Like I said, you're the better man. In time you'll understand that what you did was justified . . . And what you couldn't do was beyond your control." Seeing that his hand was shaking, and coffee slopping on to his gloves, he scowled. He could not bear the tangle of emotions welling in Jesse's eyes. Turning away, Riley grabbed the door handle. "Son," was all he could manage to say as he opened it to leave.

****

"It's been hours," sighed Catherine. "Don't you think you should . . .?"

"No." Riley cut her short. "Jesse wouldn't leave the shop unattended. He could be as upset as blazes, but he wouldn't do that. He's either out there workin' with Josiah or left him in charge before stomping out."

"But . . . He's gonna want to know that Martha Fennel's bringing Eliza down within the week. You said that's what was in the letter."

"He'll come home when he's good and ready. I'll tell him then. Don't push, Catty." Riley poured himself another lager from the pail he had filled at the brewery after leaving the shop. "The news about Eliza will do him good. Let's just eat supper now . . . Where's Theo, by the way? I haven't seen him since he lit out for school this morning."

"Missing," replied Catherine. "He shoulda been back long ago, too. I suspect . . ."

"That he's with Jesse." Riley finished her thought.

"He does worship the ground he walks on."

"As he should."

The door burst open, Jesse and Theo tumbled in. Jesse kept pummeling his younger brother, on the shoulders, on the arms, but never hard enough to inflict damage.

"Uncle," cried Theo laughing. "Uncle!"

"Uncle who?" demanded Jesse.

"Uncle Henry. Uncle Frank."

"Uncle who?"

"Uncle Val?" Theo yelled out one more relative's name.

"Jesse Cook!" reprimanded Catherine. "Leave your poor brother alone."

"What's *cooking*, Mrs. *Cook*? I'm ravenous." Jesse shoved Theo one last time before heading to the stove and the cooking pots.

"Stew," replied Catherine.

Jesse helped himself to a dripping spoonful of the bubbling gravy. Catherine waved him off, but he merely chuckled. "Army manners, Ma, which means none at all."

"Pshaw."

Riley caught Jesse's attention as he turned from the stewpot, removing his coat. "Been workin'?" Riley asked.

"Theo and I finished the lot of what you had set up . . . Sent Josiah home. Told him you'd probably work him twice as hard tomorrow . . . Queer old fellow."

"Hard enough worker, though," replied Riley. "Pickin's are kind of slim these days. Best men are in the army."

Jesse plopped down at the table beside his father. "Save any of that for me?" He tilted his head towards the pail of beer.

"Grab a mug and I'll pour you one." Riley was buoyed by his son's mood. Jesse had said his piece, displayed his anger, and appeared to be firmly back in control. He had exposed the rawest of emotions a man could admit. Riley knew they would probably never speak of it again, and that was good as far as he was concerned. Jesse must have listened. At some level he must have heard his father's words, and possibly forgiven them both.

"Thanks for your help today, Son."

"Don't think on it, Pa. I'm totally selfish. Don't want Cook & Cook to founder before I even come aboard."

Catherine was back in the room, having left momentarily. She was towing a whimpering Jimmy with one arm while holding little Willie in the other.

"What are you crying about, Jimbo?" asked Jesse.

"Washing his hands," replied Catherine.

"Washing his hands?" exclaimed Jesse. "Washing his hands? Come here, you rascal." He set down his beer, got up from the table, and flung his six-year-old brother over his shoulder. The boy began squealing and kicking. "I'll show you how we deal with dirty scoundrels in the army."

"When you're done with the scoundrel," smiled Catherine, "I've got news for you. A letter came today."

# CHAPTER 26

## The Haircut

"If we could just move the hair from this side of his head and plant it on this other side." Eliza giggled as Jesse smiled.

The other women in the room would not suppose his smile rose from the sheer joy of having his sweetheart's fingers sliding through his hair and caressing his head. *Or do they suppose?* he wondered.

He watched his mother shift her weight from one leg to another as she intently studied his head. "Try parting it about here." She pointed to an area above his left eye.

"Won't work," said Jesse. "I tried that already. My hair's used to laying the way it's used to laying."

"You're just going to have to cut it short all over," interjected Eliza's mother Martha. "I know you like wearin' it longer, Jesse, but it will grow a'gin."

Eliza leaned as close to Jesse's head as would appear proper. Even so, her bosom danced tantalizingly in front of him. *Oh, God,* he thought.

She felt the fuzz emerging around his scar and grimaced. "I'd have to cut it horribly short, Mama. Almost bald."

"Watch where you're lookin', Son." Riley had entered the kitchen. "In fact, if I were you, I'd skedaddle out o' here and find me a barber."

"Riley Cook!" Martha Fennell fumed, shaking a scissors in his direction. "Who invited you in here? Mind your manners and stay out of our business. We know what we're about."

"I thought my son's head was my business," replied Riley, suppressing a grin. "I'm the reason he's walkin' this earth . . . And since when do I have to *be invited* into my own kitchen?"

"Riley," gasped Catherine. "The things you say in mixed company . . . uh, really."

"Just remember what I said, Son. If you follow your eyeballs, this is how it will end." He nodded to Willie toddling towards him across the floor. "A household full of mewling infants and mouthy women."

"Out!" bellowed Martha to Riley's amusement. "You can . . . Catty, you're a saint among women for putting up with *that man*."

"And, Jess. When they're finished with you, I could sure use your help—if you're still able to work—in the shop." Riley was still laughing as he shut the door behind him.

Jesse squirmed. "Hand me the mirror." He looked at his reflection. "How short, Liza?"

She held up a wad of his hair, placing her fingers where the cut might be made. "About an inch?"

"Oh…"

"When you get back to your regiment you can have them cut it again. It'll even out in time," declared his mother. "You just have to keep trimming the good side to match the other."

"Oh. All right," said Jesse. "Do what you have to do, but I don't need to see it." He placed the mirror, glass down, on the table.

"You can wear your hat," said Martha.

"And a scarf," Eliza chimed in.

"You'll still be handsome in your uniform," comforted his mother.

The first locks of his hair fluttered to the floor. Jesse stared at them.

"I'll grow a mustache," he declared. "I wasn't wounded beneath my nose. Yes. I'll grow a mustache. It'll be long, bushy, a handlebar mustache. That'll keep all of you from starin' at my head."

His mother winced at the thought. Martha shook her head. Neither could imagine the very young man in front of them sporting a mustache. Not yet.

Eliza giggled as she continued to make successive cuts to his dark locks. Leaning near his good ear she whispered. "I wonder what it will feel like to kiss a man with a mustache."

Jesse could only grin in response. *Oh, you're going to like it,* he thought. His eyes told her everything she needed to know.

# CHAPTER 27

## Brothers

After weeks of recuperating, Jesse still wasn't accustomed to wearing his old trousers and colorful shirts. It had been Union blue for so long. He wouldn't part with his cavalry boots, however, even at home, and tugged them over his feet. His younger brother, Theo, watched his every move.

"Quit staring at my head," hissed Jesse, "or I'll throw you down and teach you some army justice."

"Does it still hurt?"

"Not much. A little inside from time to time."

"Did it hurt at first, when you got shot?"

"Of course, it hurt, you goose!" Jesse looked hard at his brother who seemed to have grown a foot since September. "Felt like a knife sliced through my head."

Theo plopped down on his own bed, momentarily distracted by the dog who had bounded into the room.

"Where'd you git that short-handled dog?" demanded Jesse. "He's been bothering me ever since

I came home. And how come Ma lets him in the house?"

"Don't matter that his tail's been whacked off, Jesse. He's my chum. Came into the shop one day. Wouldn't be run off. He wouldn't. Ma took to him. She's been different since you left, don't worry so much about a dog or nothin'."

"Well, keep him away from me. That tongue of his is worse than a pre-dawn wake-up, can't get a lick of sleep around here. I had to put the blanket over my head again this morning." Jesse snorted and rose to leave. The sweet smell of their mother's biscuits and freshly brewed coffee wafted up from the kitchen. He looked forward to nothing more than a solid day of labor in the shop before returning to the regiment. He had checked in at the local army headquarters earlier in the week, been issued new uniforms, and given orders to report to Richmond, Kentucky, a hundred miles south.

Theo adored his brother. He believed everything Jesse said and bragged about him throughout the neighborhood. But Theo also stood in awe of Jesse. Intimidated. Afraid of talking about what he needed to say. "Jesse, don't go."

Jesse stopped in mid-stride, glancing back at Theo. "You know I have to return to my company. I can't stay here."

"I know that . . . I mean, don't go right this minute. I need to ask you somethin'." Theo swallowed hard.

Jesse noticed the hesitation in his brother's voice, the somber expression on his face. He did not tease or dismiss Theo, but plopped back on the bed, granting him his full attention. "So. Talk."

"Do you like being in the army?"

"Sometimes. I like being a noncom. That's what they call us sergeants and corporals. I like having responsibility and leading men when I can. I don't like being hungry, cold, filthy dirty, or so tired you could sleep standing up."

"Have you killed anybody?"

*That's what this is about,* Jesse thought. His mind flashed back to the first time he had knowingly taken another man's life. The crimson stains on his blue coat. The sounds of death. The fear. Gagging on his own vomit. Nothing he was up to sharing with Theo.

"You want to know if your brother kills people? What? You wanna brag on it?" Jesse regretted the words as soon as he said them. Theo's earnest face was reddening before his eyes. Jesse rubbed the stubble on his chin. He had to choose his words more carefully. "Theo, when I wanted to join up, Pa told me . . ." Jesse paused, forcing himself to state aloud (again) things he would rather suppress. "Pa told me that there was nothing glorious about killing a man. He was right. There's nothing good about it at all. I'm a soldier, and I've done what soldiers have to do. It can be honorable. But, it's mostly ugly—the killin' part."

Theo didn't move. He kept holding his dog, kept gazing at Jesse as if expecting more.

*I hate the way he puts me on a Golderned pedestal,* thought Jesse. "I was taught to shoot in the army," he continued, searching for appropriate words. "Taught to ride, how to act under fire . . . tactics and maneuvers." He paused, looked compassionately at his brother, and gently said, "The answer to your question, Theo, is . . . yes. It's nothing to be proud of, though. It's just something that had to be done."

A palpable silence fell between them. Jesse wondered what to do. *God this is torture. Why isn't he leaving? Should I?* He opted to stay, waiting his brother out.

Theo finally spoke, too loudly, as if volume would give him courage. "I asked Pa to sign for me to enlist, Jesse. I'm bigger and stronger than I used to be and almost as old as . . ."

"Tarnation, Theo!" Jesse exploded off the bed. "No! Absolutely not. NO! Never. Pa refused, right? He said *no*?"

"I was hopin' you'd talk to him," stammered Theo, reddening, jarred by Jesse's words.

Their mother's voice interrupted them. "Anything wrong up there? It sounds a wee stormy."

"No, Ma," yelled Jesse. "It's just Theo's damned, er, darned dog."

"Oh, Jesse," Catherine replied shaking her head. "You two hurry down here."

Jesse lowered his voice and spoke pointedly to his brother. "It's not about how strong you are, or how big you are. It's about how important you are." He gripped his brother's shoulders with both hands, holding him firmly, forcing him to pay attention to the pent-up, half-buried words now spilling forth.

"It's about my chum Pete dying before my eyes, nothing but blood and gore where his arm and leg should have been. It's about not being able to save him, or even bring him home. Pete lies now, not in a proper cemetery where his folks can go and pay respects, but in an unmarked grave on some field in Virginia. Is that what you want, Theo? It's not some grand adventure."

Jesse dropped his arms, eyes threatening to tear. He walked to the window and began to aimlessly scratch the frost from the pane with his fingernails. "It's not what I want for my little brother." The scratching was aimless; his back hunched. "You don't know the half of it . . . I've never told anyone, 'cept Pa, how scared I was most of the time. We all were. If I was a smarter man, I'd figure out a way to end it." He turned to face his brother. "Promise me that you will not run off and do somethin' reckless. Promise me, Theo. Swear it. Let me do my duty. As the eldest son, it is *my* duty."

Theo swallowed. He could not speak and felt uncomfortable with his brother's revelations. The pain in Jesse's eyes was unbearable. The mere thought that Jesse could be scared horrified him. He had no idea what to say.

Jesse cleared his throat, standing straighter, regaining his composure. "Tomorrow I'm leaving. I don't know what faces me. I do know that I'm trusting you to stay here and care for the family, our shop, Ma . . . even Pa. All of them. I need you to step up and do that, Theo. Will you? Please."

"Yeah, I promise." Theo sighed in relief, called for his dog and started to back away, intending to escape by descending to breakfast. Jesse stopped him.

"There's one more thing. I do admire your desire to enlist, Theo. I do." He paused, allowing those words to resonate. "Listen. I heard some officers talking a while back. When this war's over, there'll be a need for local militias to guarantee the peace, especially in border states like Kentucky. We have men fighting on both sides, and there will be deep feelings one way or the other." Jesse offered his hand to his brother. "When that time comes, I will be at the head of the line." He smiled at Theo. "I would be proud to have you ride by my side then."

Theo returned his brother's smile and handshake. "I'd be proud to, Corporal."

"That's my boy. But when this militia forms, I expect to get myself a higher rank than corporal." Jesse grinned and threw his arm around Theo's shoulders. "Should we ask Pa to join up with us?"

"He's pretty old. Do you think he can fight?"

"Oh, yeah," Jesse laughed. "I wouldn't want to go up against him."

# CHAPTER 28

**Richmond, Kentucky**
**February 1865**

Jesse wasn't the only soldier on the Lexington train the morning he returned. Sometimes it seemed like every able-bodied man under forty was in uniform, on some military errand or the other.

They had wanted to suit him out in a completely new uniform at the Covington barracks. He appreciated the gloves, greatcoat, and trousers. The latter actually fit, unlike the pair he had wound up wearing from the hospital. He liked the sharp new Hardee hat and kepi. But the boots and jacket he respectfully declined. His boots were comfortably stretched and molded to his feet. He wasn't about to give them up until the soles wore through.

The jacket—If they had forced him to accept a new one, he swore he would have left it behind. His ma had done a credible job of cleaning his old jacket. The stains were still visible, but muted. That jacket was Jesse, his badge of honor, and he wasn't about to part with it.

The last bursts of steam were escaping the engine, washing over the station platform as he bounded down the steps from the car. *Now I just have to figure out where the 53rd is headquartered.*

A recognizable voice surprised and delighted him, for he had not expected to be met.

"You look a sight better than when I saw you last," remarked Stu. He strode confidently across the platform to embrace his comrade. Jesse responded in kind.

"So do you," he replied. "Barracks life good?"

"It's a solid building, Jesse. Brick. Stoves in the rooms, and the wind doesn't whistle through every crack and crevice. You're gonna like it."

Jesse hoisted his meager gear onto his shoulder. "Much of a walk from here?"

"Not when you have a horse."

"Pretty?"

"She's waitin' for ya, but not just yet. I put them in livery." Stu grinned. "We need to celebrate your return, Chum. How about a smooth drink and a hearty meal? The hotel there has a fine restaurant."

"Hotel restaurant?" chuckled Jesse. "You been lucky at dice?"

"Took up a collection. The whole company wanted you welcomed back in style."

"I'll be Golderned," was all Jesse could think to say.

****

"I feel like a stuffed hog." He pushed back from the table and sighed with pleasure, his beer in hand.

"Enjoy it while you can," laughed Stu. "Our successful raid into Virginia did not improve the skill or attitude of the cooks."

Jesse had spent the bulk of the meal telling his fellow corporal about his recuperation in Covington, his days spent in the cooper shop, and his haircutting travails. The details of his conversations with his father and brother he kept to himself. "So, you've heard all about me. What's going on with the regiment?"

"Well, you know they split us up. Nobody really knows why, and in typical army fashion, they're not about to tell us. My guess is they're thinkin' we can be spread out thin 'cause there's not much of a threat. Anyways, we're stationed here. Company D's at Mt. Sterling. F was sent to Camp Nelson. I don't know about the others."

"Have you been out patrollin'?"

"Not really. We've barely settled in. I suppose we'll start soon. The guerrillas aren't whipped."

"Those same fellas?"

"Yep. Your namesake Mr. Jessee. Webster. Mundy. They're all still out there."

"Tarnation. Maybe too many of us went to Virginia."

"Jesse, were you able to see Jim?" Stu leaned forward on the table, his hands cradling his stein of beer.

"Just before I left Covington. You know they sawed his foot off."

"Yeah."

"He's going to live. I guess he's lucky in that. He was spared the gangrene. . . But, Stu, he's not good in his head. How could he be? I'm not all good in mine either, as you witnessed."

Stu cleared his throat. "But you're doin' better. Jim's a fine lad. He's gotta get to that point."

"I know. I wish I coulda helped him more. He's learnin' to walk with a crutch and he might get some kind of peg, but . . . I don't know what kind of work he can do without being able to walk right. He could handle a wagon. I suggested that to him, but with most rigs he's going to be expected to jump out and help load. If he's goin' to work at all he has to learn to hobble around fast and sure."

"Could be a clerk somewhere," said Stu, "but he can't read well. What does his father do to earn a wage?"

"Laborer, and what you need for that is a strong body. That's all Jimmy knows, Stu."

"When this is over, we gotta figure out some way to help him."

"Yeah. I'll keep thinkin' on it. Maybe between the two of us . . . So, how are the rest of the boys?"

"We all got frostbite on the ride back from Virginia, nearly every member of the 53$^{rd}$, and some pretty badly. No one else in our platoon had to have anything amputated, thank God, but a couple were hospitalized in Lexington. We all have toes and fingers that still don't work so good."

Jesse let out a slow breath, leaning back in his chair, relaxed from the effect of the alcohol. "While I was home I read in the paper about a Lt. Morin drowning while crossing the Clinch River. I didn't really know him, did you? But I certainly remember that nightmare of a crossing."

"How could you forget? And, no, I never had any business with him."

"Well, as it turns out," Jesse continued. "He shows up back in Covington—alive—appears he didn't drown after all, but was captured by the Rebs and then released."

"That's amazing. Can you imagine falling in that water and surviving? Rebs must have been right there and pulled him out . . . How come nobody on our side saw any of this?"

"Don't know. He must have washed downstream a-ways." Jesse finished his beer, then stared into the stein, debating if he should order another. "Seven of our boys died in the hospitals in Covington while I was home, Stu. If you add that number to those we left behind . . ." He couldn't go on, would not speak of Pete. He shook his head sadly. "I hope we do nothing here, nothing at all. Just polish our boots. I wish this whole damnable thing was over."

\*\*\*\*

They dismounted in the dirt alley beside the army stables. Jesse had done nothing but stroke and pat Pretty's head and neck the entire ride from the depot. Now that he was off her back, she was returning the favor, nuzzling him to distraction.

"Yeah, she missed you," said Stu.

Jesse chortled, "I have a way with women."

Stu took the reins from Jesse's hand. "Well, Romeo, why don't you go in and greet your squad? I'll take care of Juliet."

Jesse shot Stu a questioning look.

"No, go on," Stu insisted. "You won't have any trouble finding them. Through that double door in the front, up the stairs, to the right. We're all quartered on the second floor. They should be in there this time of day . . . Go!"

Jesse began to untie his gear. Stu stopped him. "I'll bring that stuff, too. Go!"

"Okay. Thanks." Jesse smiled broadly, adjusted his Hardee hat over his shortly cropped hair and nearly ran to the barracks entrance. After showing his orders to the desk clerk, and warmly greeting a few familiar faces, he bounded up the stairs two at a time.

In his eagerness, Jesse didn't bother to knock. He simply burst through the door. He scanned the room, taking in every detail, absorbing the scene—his squad, his boys—there, before him, behaving perfectly ordinary. Danny and Charley were working at a table, busily cleaning gear. Johnny was stoking the fire in the stove. Joe appeared to be writing a letter. "Mein Gott," he uttered, "Corporal Jesse. I t'ought I'd never see you again."

"Joe," Jesse said warmly. "Johnny. Charley. Danny." He looked at them each in turn, delighted to just *see* them again, but he needed to break the trance. "Why are you all just standing there? Is it the hair?" He feigned embarrassment.

It was as if he had released them from some military protocol. Johnny was the first to reach his side, slamming the stove door in such haste that he had to stomp out a burning ember that had been thrown free. Almost immediately, Johnny was joined by both Charley and Danny. They slapped Jesse on the back, threw arms around his shoulders, hugged him in turn, and in the process knocked off his hat.

"Woah, what a scar," remarked Charley.

"Will Mis Liza still pine for you now that yer half bald?" baited Danny.

"Eliza admires me for what's inside my head, my brain, not what's on top."

"Oh, yeah, sure," Danny laughed. "She was really admiring your brain back there in Ohio last fall."

Jesse smiled broadly, "Of course she was." To change the subject, he turned his attention to Johnny who hadn't taken his eyes off him. "Tarnation. You're as annoying as my real little brother." He playfully swatted their youngest member, shoving him down on a cot. "It's so good to see all of you. Bully. You must tell me everything that's happened."

His eyes shot to Joe, who had not joined the others in the euphoric reunion. Joe simply stood there, next to the cot where he had been seated writing. "Joe," said Jesse crossing the room, "Thank you." He sensed that the big man was overcome with emotion, and offered his hand. "Thank you—for everything."

Joe grabbed Jesse's hand in both of his, then dropped it and practically broke his ribs in an exuberant embrace. He began jabbering in excited German, then switched to English. "Vas can I do for you, Corporal? Vould you like to sit? Need something to eat? Vas bed do you want? Dis one?"

"Slow down, Joe. I'm good. I'm feeling hunkey dorey, and I just ate—a feast. Golderned, it's good to be back."

"And it's good to have *you* back." Sergeant Blackwood had entered the room unnoticed. "Stu told me I might find you here." He quickly closed the space between them to shake Jesse's hand. "Welcome back, Jesse."

"Sergeant."

"And you're just in time. We're about to have a briefing. . . It's back to work, Corporal."

Jesse grabbed his Hardee off the floor, flicked dirt from the brim, and squared it once more on his head. "I never thought anything about the army would be music to my ears," he grinned, "but *back to work* sounds mighty good."

# CHAPTER 29

**March, 1865**

Jesse eyed Stu across the table in the barracks kitchen. "That was one interesting briefing," he said. "Mundy's finally been captured—the first to fall. Bully for the 30<sup>th</sup> Wisconsin."

"Yeah," Stu replied. "He'll be hanged before you know it, as a common thug."

"The Union can't regard that sodomite devil as a rightful soldier or prisoner of war." Jesse took a swig of his coffee, now cold. "I didn't like hearin' bout that other fellow takin' up where Mundy left off, though."

"What'd they say he did again? I'm losin' track of all these guerrillas. I just wish we'd come across one of 'em in action. Show 'em what the 53<sup>rd</sup> can do."

"He raided a railroad south of Louisville. Derailed it. Robbed the passengers and burned the cars." *And he has the same name as my ma, uncle, and grandmother. Good God. Another Gentry.* "I feel like we're not accomplishing much here, Stu. All day today I did nothin' but stand behind the counter in a dry goods store and watch Confederate deserters register with the Provost Marshall's office so they wouldn't be taken for spies or guerrillas. I would look at their faces and want to kill them. What are we doin', just welcoming them back?"

Stu sighed and shook his head. "I'm with you, Jesse. You just wonder if they're not gonna go right back out tonight and join up with some roving band . . . And when we walk down the street."

"I feel like I'm in Richmond, *Virginia*. The people here don't even consider me and you *Kentuckians.* Covington—Newport—too close to Ohio. We don't even *sound* like they do, as I've been told."

"And who wants to *draaawl* like that. Takes 'em a month of Sundays to tell ya anything."

Blackwood slid down the bench to join in his corporals' conversation. "Boys, I hear ya, but keep your feelings in this room. We don't need to rattle the troops. Tomorrow our platoon's riding. We're to sweep for guerrillas and horse thieves."

"Horse thieves," scoffed Jesse. "No wonder. I read in the paper that the government's buying them for up to $175 per head for the army, and they prob'ly don't ask questions. Makes you want to sleep in the stables. Some bastard who's registered might steal our mounts and sell them back to us."

"That's why you boys post guards every blessed night."

"How're we supposed to catch horse thieves?" growled Stu.

"Respond to complaints. Take descriptions. And follow those leads to the government posts if we have to."

"They're going to love us," Jesse laughed, "waltzin' in there, saying 'Oh, by the way, you government boys just paid good money for that horse which we are now going to take and return to poor Farmer John.'" He looked soberly at the sergeant. "Sometimes this *peace-keeping* is a tougher duty than linin' up for battle. I don't even know who the enemy is, man, woman, or child."

"It wouldn't be much better if we were HQ'd back home," Blackwood replied. "I heard a guerrilla is recruiting for the Confederate Army in Kenton County even as amnesty is being granted."

"Makes no sense. They could swear, sign, and join up again."

"We're all kind of jittery," continued the sergeant. "It's to be expected. Grant's got Lee on the ropes. Just a matter of time . . . But these southern boys aren't gonna go down easy. . . Heard one of the 55th boys was bayoneted by his own guard—killed— when he failed to halt. Turns out the fella was just sleepwalking. Jittery all 'round, I'd say."

"Golderned."

"One more thing. We haven't been officially assigned this duty, but prepare yourselves. Don't tell your boys yet. Orders are coming down to investigate pawnbrokers and secondhand shops for receiving and selling used soldiers' uniforms, revolvers, swords, you name it. Such trade is forbidden."

"Just one more thing to endear us to the local populace. Either of you want another cup of coffee?"

"Oh, God, no, Jesse. That stuff is rotting your gut right through."

Jesse grinned wickedly. "Maybe I'll get lucky, and me and my rotting gut will be sent home to rest and recuperate with Liza."

"When your gut rots," said Blackwood in the same lighthearted vein, "I'll see to it that *you* recuperate at the local civilian hospital, nursed by slow talkin' southern sympathizin' women—old ones."

# CHAPTER 30

**April 4, 1865**
**Covington, Kentucky**

Riley was half-dressed. Pre-dawn. It was still dark, but the cannon fire had awakened him. *Cannon fire?* he thought. He quickly laced his shoes, yanked on a shirt, snapped his braces in place, and groped for the doorway. Catherine was right behind him, not bothering with street clothes. She simply threw her shawl over her dressing gown.

"Pa!" Theo made it to the hallway ahead of his father. "What's goin' on? Are the Rebs attackin'?"

"Slip out, Son. Keep to the shadows but find out. I'll be mindin' the shop." Theo bolted before Catherine found the words to object.

This was exciting. Theo felt empowered: his job, his mission, for his pa. As first light began to disperse the darkness, he caught glimpses of other boys, other men, and even a few women filtering from doorways—some half-dressed—searching for answers.

*Those aren't just cannons,* he thought. *That's musket fire, too.*

As he ventured from their alley, rounding the corner to head towards the river, he saw what he thought was the sunrise. Only it wasn't. The sky over Cincinnati was aglow from what appeared to be fire.

More people. Shouting now. And the closer he got to the river, the louder it grew. He caught bits and pieces of conversation, first cautious and then jubilant.

"What in blazes is happenin' out there?"

"Who's firin'?"

"At who?"

"It ain't no invasion. I'm tellin' ya."

"Where in tarnation is the Army when you need them?"

A grizzled man with a prominent limp and few teeth slapped Theo on the back, startling him. "It's a celebration, boy. Not a battle. Our General Grant has taken Richmond. This here war will soon be over . . . And General Lee a dead man."

"Richmond?" It took Theo a moment to process. "Richmond, Virginia?"

"Of course, Virginia, boy." The man gave him a disgusted look. "Wha'd you think? You *simple* or sumthin'?"

*Not where Jesse is. Good. That old fellow probably doesn't even know there's such a place as Richmond, Kentucky.* Theo smiled, relieved. *Gotta get home and spread the news.*

He had made his way as far as the market place. It was getting more difficult to walk. People were streaming in from all directions—seemingly, the entire town. He had never seen anything like it and was momentarily distracted from heading back. A bonfire was erupting, men and boys tossing anything that would burn into its mass. The pile soon blazed in celebratory rage.

"Theo. Theo Cook." He heard his name being called, looked towards the sound, and spotted a chum from school. "Help us out, Theo." The boy and a few others were tugging desperately at a large piece of driftwood, hauling it up from the river. He was set to take shoulder to it himself when the realization of what he was witnessing bore down upon him.

Men were now heaving empty barrels into the flames, even good lumber (no doubt stolen from the nearby yard). Benches. Chairs. "My God," he said aloud. "I've gotta warn Pa."

Theo was a fast runner and needed to prove it now. People were fanning out in search of wood to add to the conflagration. He wove his way through them, pushing when he had to, more than one fist shaking in his direction as he passed. Only once did he pause, and that was in sheer amazement. Some townsmen had commandeered an entire battery of six-pound cannon and gunpowder—moving it relentlessly towards the square.

As he rounded the corner back into his own alley, he saw his father propped up against the shop doors, which were still locked and bolted. Riley was holding his ancient musket, which Theo figured must have belonged to some relative during the War of 1812, it was so old. "Pa!"

"Catch your breath, Son. I already heard. It's a *good* day."

"But did you know?" Theo was gasping, doubled over, trying to do just what his father had told him and catch his breath. He stood erect quickly enough. "There's rowdies. They're lookin' for barrels, wood . . . anything that'll burn . . . huge bonfire . . . and fellows with cannon."

The six-pounders boomed for the first time. Then again. Again. Windows rattled. One in the building directly opposite the shop shattered, sending shards in their direction. "Sonofabitch," growled Riley. "Damned fools're gonna start a riot."

A few strange men had come storming 'round the corner into the alley. They were unsavory in appearance, one even sporting a souvenir Confederate Army jacket. Riley quickly appraised them, motioning for Theo to go around back. "Bring out a few buckets, some staves, nothin' finished mind you . . . that busted keg. And hurry." As his son did as he was told, Riley muttered, "We'll contribute to the cause."

He remained where he stood, not moving an inch, ready to greet his fellow townsmen, gun-in-hand. He watched them make their way down the alley. They yanked at loose fence posts and scanned yards, looking for easy pickings.

"Gen-tle-men." He drew out the syllables for emphasis. "You're just who I was waitin' for." He moved his palm ever so slowly over the butt of the musket, caressing it. "How 'bout giving my son a hand . . . addin' the stuff he'll be bringin' out to the bonfire." He gestured towards Theo who was running back to the rear of the shop after dumping his first hastily gathered load on the ground.

Two of the men immediately began scooping up the buckets and staves. The third kept his eye on Riley's musket, wary.

"Just worried there might be Reb deserters about," said Riley. "Sympathizers. Can't be too careful."

"No, ye can't." The man, who appeared to be the ringleader, motioned for the other two to get moving. Seeing Theo arrive with the keg, he shouldered that himself, and turned to face Riley. "You oughta come down yerself. Bring the boy, yer missus . . . *and* yer musket. We're celebratin'."

"Maybe I will."

As the men hightailed it up the alley, Riley aimed the musket skyward and fired. Theo nearly fell to the ground. "Blazes!" His grin said it all. "Just . . . Tarnation!"

"No need them thinkin' the old girl won't fire," chortled Riley. "Or that we ain't givin' enough."

**Richmond, Kentucky**
**The Following Day**

Jesse continued reading the headlines aloud to his platoon, each one met with a rousing "huzzah" and another drink from the whiskey which flooded the barracks.

## The Great Victory
## Lee Retreating to Lynchburg
## His Forces Melting Away
## Occupation of Richmond
## The President in Jefferson Davis' House
## Fifteen Thousand Rebel Prisoners

"To the Union," toasted Sergeant Blackwood.

"The Army of the Potomac," Johnny said.

"Huzzah!"

"Well done, boys," bellowed Charley.

"Mr. Lincoln," offered Stu.

"The Union."

"To boredom and polishing boots," Jesse belched, "forever."

"And to the ladies back home," said Danny raising his glass one more time.

The door flew open. Their company lieutenant, not too steady on his own feet, stumbled through. "Boys!" he thundered. "Orders from the War Department. A salute of 100 guns in honor of the capture of Richmond will be fired at meridian the day after the receipt of this order at each military post and arsenal in the United States."

"Hip, hip." Someone started the cheer again.

"Hurrah!"

"Hip, hip."

Glasses and cups clanked together. Whiskey flowed freely, slopping onto the floor, onto cots, onto uniforms.

Jesse leaped up on a chair, nearly upsetting it, which met with a boisterous roar from his comrades. "To the 53rd!" He held his now nearly-empty glass aloft in tribute. "To all of us . . . to Pete."

"Hear, hear," called out the lieutenant.

"To us," Joe said softly.

"And to Jim," whispered Stu, offering the toast back to Jesse.

# CHAPTER 31

**April 15, 1865**
**Richmond, Kentucky**

The last week had been nothing short of amazing as far as Jesse was concerned. Exciting. He found it difficult to maintain interest in routine day-to-day soldiering. The war was clearly ending. Soon they *must* be ordered home for good.

General Lee had finally surrendered the Army of Northern Virginia to General Grant—at some little town that Jesse had never heard of, Appomattox Courthouse. It was just a matter of time before the rest of the Confederates surrendered, those armies still active in Georgia and farther west.

People throughout the Union had celebrated long and loud upon receiving the news from Virginia. They set off rockets and lit bonfires far into the night. Cannons boomed. Engine houses rang their bells, and church bells pealed. It was glorious.

Most symbolic of all, the United States flag was once again flying over Fort Sumter in Carolina, where the first shots of the war had been fired back in '61.

Jesse had been told that in Covington and Newport nearly every house was decorated with flags and patriotic bunting. Townsfolk fired their guns in salute, and bands played in the streets. Every day he checked for letters from home which would describe the goings-on in detail.

Would Pa again have fired that ancient musket? Theo had written earlier in the month about their father scaring off would-be rowdies. A smile crossed Jesse's face as he laid down his now-gleaming Colt revolver and glanced at the carbine standing by the barracks door. *Now these are fine weapons,* he thought. *I don't think I'd feel safe firing that relic.*

He pushed back in his chair, tilting it on the hind legs—the front feet lightly pressing on his boots. He was leaning against the wall near his cot, extremely satisfied. In their daily briefing they had heard even more good news. The guerrilla leaders Colonel George Jessee and Moses Webster had made offers to surrender upon the same terms as Lee and Grant. Each of their men would give up his arms and horses . . .

*Gotta get goin'. Find the boys—Stu—change the guard.* He glanced at his pocket watch, then stood to grab his jacket and strap on his revolver.

He heard pounding footsteps in the hall, shouts. *Something's happening. Hurry.* He neglected the jacket buttons, hastily buckled the belt, squared his Hardee on his head and sprinted towards the door. Before he could reach it, however, Stu threw it open from the hallway side. He was pale and shaken.

"Jesse," he blurted, his face contorted, "Someone shot the President. Last night. In Washington. Just came over the wire. Some Southern bastard killed Mr. Lincoln."

## Cincinnati, Ohio

Eliza tossed the bloody rags into the trash pit. They were disgusting—too wet, too red. She couldn't begin to wash them. Her hands . . . those she must clean. She rammed the pump handle up, then down, up, down, and again, until the cold soothing liquid began to rinse away the remnants of her cousin's birthing ordeal.

Everything was wrong. The baby seemed too scrawny, the mother too weak. Her own mother had shooed Eliza from the room on this errand. The child was cursed. Any child born on this day would certainly be cursed. In a matter of hours the nation had plummeted from hopeful and jubilant to shock, despair, hatred.

She looked at her now-gleaming hands and leaned against the well casing, feeling old for her sixteen years, and a bit chilled on this early spring afternoon. She had come outside without her cloak, not wanting to stain it with the blood. It was bad enough that her apron was stained. The apron she could not afford to throw into the pit, though. Ripping it off, she crumbled it in a wad. She would find a pan and soak it clean.

This was the second birth she was privileged to attend. It was sobering and magical and dreadful all at once. This time, though, had not been as easy as the first. Even her mother's concoctions of herbs and ointments didn't ease the problems. Complications they called them. Why, her mother had practically reached in and ripped that baby out.

"Jesse," Eliza whispered, wrapping her arms about herself for warmth. "Jesse. Do you know about this cursed day? Until today, I expected to hear you'd be coming home. The South has surrendered. General Lee surrendered. . . But, now. This. They've shot Mr. Lincoln. What will they order you to do?"

The door opened and Cousin America, a girl of about eight—the newborn's oldest sibling—stepped quietly into the yard.

"Come here." Eliza opened her arms invitingly. The girl fairly raced into the embrace, hugging Eliza around the waist and burying her face in the folds of her frock. America's young body immediately began to warm Eliza.

"Is my Mama gonna die?" The child was trembling slightly and beginning to sob.

"What makes you say such a thing, Dear? Has somebody said something? Only God decides about dying."

"Nobody says nothin', or comes out neither. I can't hear nothin' through the door."

Eliza stroked the girl's hair, pushing it back from her forehead. "Spyin', huh?" She smiled. "I'd be spyin', too. Sit with me." The two of them settled onto a roughhewn bench.

"My ma has helped many, many mothers have babies," Eliza continued. "Sometimes babies are sickly for a while, but most do okay. Look at you. You were a baby once and you're getting big and strong now. Look at your brother."

"And the mamas?"

"Sometimes they are sickly for a while, too. They just need to rest." Eliza did not release the girl's hand, the better to comfort her. "In a minute we'll go in and I'll find out for you how your mama is. Without spyin'."

They turned their attention to some passersby on the street.

"Do they know Mama?"

"I don't know. Prob'ly not. Why?"

"They look sad, too."

"They're sad for another reason, America. Do you know who Abraham Lincoln is?"

"Of course, I do. He's the Pres'dent . . . of the whole United States."

"Well," Eliza cleared her throat. "Those people are sad, and I am sad, because President Lincoln died today."

"Did he have the fever?"

"No, he was killed by an evil man. He was shot with a gun, just like our brave soldiers."

Eliza's mother Martha thrust her head out of an upstairs window. "Liza," she called. "We need that after-birthin' tea brewed quick as you can; and, America, sweetheart, your mother would like to see you now."

Liza gave the girl another squeeze and sent her off. Since she was bidden to fix tea, the crisis must be waning. She sincerely hoped that was the case.

Walking into the kitchen, Eliza wanted this day to end better than it had begun. She wanted her cousin and that tiny baby to live and thrive. She yearned to marry her Jesse and bear his babies, and someday she swore that she would. A year from now? Two? This war could not last forever. She thought of the stirring prose that had filled the afternoon paper. She thought of the sacrifices that they had all borne: herself, Jesse, their families, the wounded, the dead, her own martyred and wounded uncles, Jesse's friend Pete.

*This war was not fought just to have Mr. Lincoln die,* she lamented. *It is unspeakable. Surely, there is a reason. This horror must result in something. It was fought for a reason. Surely. . . something better.*

*Our children.* The thought steadied her as she reached for a pitcher. *Our babies will have it better than this. As Jesse and I live and breathe, I swear it. We will make it better for our children.* She crossed herself and muttered a prayer.

# CHAPTER 32

## To the Cumberland Gap
## May 1865

This ride was different. The worst of them were better horsemen, lighter on the reins, more stable in the saddle, a smoother gait. The best of them were superb, seemingly one with the horse. But it was not that which struck those who saw them pass. There was no gaiety in this ride, no sense of great adventure. The men rode without fanfare, their faces solemn. They were seasoned veterans, riding in response to the murder of their president. No one would dare cross them.

They were four companies strong: Jesse's Company B from the 53rd Kentucky, two other companies from Mt. Sterling, and Company E of the 185th Ohio. Under orders from General Hobson in Lexington they were to move immediately to the Cumberland Gap on the Kentucky/Tennessee border—the senior officers from Ohio assuming command.

Events had moved swiftly since the President's assassination. Uncertainty, rumor, fatigue, and tension plagued both the army and the civilian populace. Jesse knew that many depredations were being committed near the Tennessee line by citizen guerrillas. That's all they heard in their daily briefings, and they were headed there now. All manner of bands of Southern sympathizers and angry Rebel soldiers who denied defeat were on the loose throughout Kentucky. It was the mission on this ride to scout the country and break up these guerrilla bands if encountered. They had been given seven days' rations of sugar, coffee, meat, and hard bread. After that amount of time, he supposed, they were to have reached the Cumberland Gap where they would relieve troops already stationed there.

They had been instructed to respect the private property of citizens and to issue proper receipts and vouchers for forage. Any prisoners were to be forwarded to headquarters in Lexington. Jesse could still hear his captain reading the concluding words of the order at their briefing, "It is expected that your command will behave as true soldiers, patriots, and gentlemen." *Gentlemen,* he thought. *That's a far cry from the way we entered Virginia.*

"Maybe anybody out there will just surrender to us," said Stu, who was riding within earshot of Jesse.

"I was talkin' to one of the boys from the 39th last night," replied Jesse. "They were involved in that big surrender near Mt. Sterling before coming here. One thousand men surrendering. Maybe more. Can you imagine that? They weren't sure it was gonna work out all right."

"There was prob'ly more Rebs than us."

"Couple companies at Mt. Sterling. That was all we had when they waltzed in with a white flag seeking terms. This fella said they sent units from Covington and Big Sandy to back up our boys, to get in the rear of the Rebs."

"Golderned. I hope we don't come across anything like that. Who were they, by the way? You know?"

"Forces of General Basil Duke—Morgan's men."

"The best of the guerrillas."

"Yeah, the best of the worst," growled Jesse. Shifting his attention from Stu, he looked back at the long line of troopers. It would be time soon to make camp. *I can't tell you this, Stu. You might take it wrong, but Eliza thinks . . . No, Eliza knows that one of her cousins rode with Morgan. Maybe he surrendered—the son of a bitch. Or maybe he's dead . . . Strange war. Cousins fighting cousins.*

The oddest thing about this first day's ride had been the people they passed—civilians, coloreds, paroled Southern soldiers—all on the move, heading somewhere. And they were a sorry lot. Dirty. Corpse-thin. Sullen. The troopers had stopped and questioned some of them, the groups with the most males, men wearing remnants of battle grey, the healthiest and angriest looking of the lot.

One fellow had shouted at them, "We are not whipped yet. One Confederate is equal to five Yankees, as the war has proved." This caused a stir among the men who heard it and only the firm hand of their officers kept the fellow safe from being thrashed or worse. None of these people seemed particularly threatening. They weren't armed, just annoyingly self-righteous, arrogant, and belligerent.

****

"Jesse, have you seen this?" Sergeant Blackwood was waving a newspaper in his direction. It was almost dark, but their bonfire gave enough light to read by.

"What is it, Sarge?"

"A copy of the *Gazette* from home. From a week or so back. This part just got my ire and made me laugh. Good men of Covington. Reminded me of today." Blackwood tapped the article he wanted his corporal to read.

*Rebel uniforms may be seen on every corner and in every hotel and barroom in Covington. The wearers are, for the most part, quite jolly, and seem to be pretty well supplied with gold and silver, some of it stolen, no doubt. The impudent talk of these men very naturally excites the ire of loyal men, and it is not an uncommon thing to see a Johnny stretched at full length upon the pavement in consequence of coming in contact with a Union man's fist. The appearance of a rebel uniform has about the same effect upon one of our loyal citizens—well known for his muscular power—as the sight of a red rag produces upon an infuriated bull.*

Jesse finished reading and motioned for Blackwood to sit beside him. "Tarnation. Maybe they are all going North."

"I just wonder if any of the muscular loyal citizens are friends of ours."

"Probably my Pa," chuckled Jesse. "He's a brawler from way back." He glanced again at the paper, farther down on the page. "Look at this. It says *General Stoneman* sent 39 Rebel officers, 483 soldiers, and 22 political prisoners through Cincinnati on their way to Camp Chase. Captured them in North Carolina. I heard rumors he was on another raid. Guess it's true."

"Guess it is. Kind of wish I was with him. At least they're still facing a known enemy, not packs of former Rebs who are now *civilians*."

"I think I have a cousin riding with Stoneman, Sarge. Hope he's okay. Artillery man. Name's Ben."

"Artillery. That's power. Don't know if I'd want to be one, though."

Danny had joined them. "Couldn't help but overhearin'. How are we supposed to deal with an enemy who has surrendered but doesn't act like it? How? My grandmother wrote that the recent fires in Newport were believed set by Rebels returning home from the war. They gonna burn down their own town?"

"It's gonna be bad for a while," said Jesse. "But in time things'll work out. I hope. We won't always be askin' of men we meet, you Reb or Loyal, will we? Anytime we drink with a fella in a bar? Fellows we might work with?"

****

Jesse lay on his bedroll the longest time, unable to sleep. The night air was sweet with Kentucky spring, with a soft Southern warmth. It felt good, comforting, so unlike the winter just past. That deadly cold was mere months ago but felt like years. Everything had changed and so fast. The war was officially over. The President was buried and a new one inaugurated. Jesse still wasn't used to saying President Johnson. It sounded strange, wrong. There was already talk that General Grant should become president. Jesse liked the sound of that. Very much. Grant was an Ohio man, born near Ripley where Liza lived. Mrs. Grant had lived in Covington during much of the war. Big house. A mansion. Jesse knew where it was.

Eliza. . . How he yearned for that girl. Those curls. That smile. The way she melted every part of him with a mere touch. He smiled in the dark. *Yes, she is my cher bebe.* He had not laid on her since that first time. There had been no way, no privacy when he was home. Besides, he did not want to have her be with child before she should. There was always that risk, even with protection. *As soon as I get home I must marry that girl. Ask her proper. Set up a date. Find some minister. In Ripley. It should be where she lives. That's how it's done.*

His mind wandered to images of Eliza, fantasies. He imagined Eliza in the kitchen, Eliza bringing him breakfast, Eliza in his bed, Eliza with his baby, and him off in his cooper shop making money hand over fist. *'Cause Jesse Cook will be there as the nation gears up for a new age. Whatever opportunities are out there, I will seize. For Eliza . . .* He had no doubt about his abilities, his future, or his manhood. He was twenty years old now, his birthday coming on this very ride. And they had just won a war.

His last conscious thought before sleep was noting the call of a whippoorwill—longing for a mate.

****

The next days were much like the first: traveling southeast, questioning groups of Confederate parolees, making camp, then moving on again. They encountered no obvious bands of guerrillas, no one particularly threatening. The scouts had reported on criminal activity, horse thievery, robbery, looting of the civilian populace, but the perpetrators were phantom-like—always two or three steps ahead of the army.

"When I get home," said Danny, who now rode in Pete's former position next to Jesse. "I wanna find me a woman."

"Hope you do. Wear your uniform as long as you can. They have an uncanny effect on the ladies." Jesse grinned mischievously. "Remember Grandma?"

"Well, I would like someone under fifty, or forty," Danny muttered.

"Ha, ha. Hey, Joe," Jesse yelled. "Know any nice girls you can introduce to Danny? English speaking preferred."

"German women are *sehr gut*. Take good care of a man. Cooking. Cleaning."

"What about the important things?" teased Jesse.

"That, too," laughed Joe. "Just . . . They can be, vas *ist* da word? Bossy."

"Then stay away from them, Danny," advised Jesse. "Who wants a bossy woman? Might as well stay in the army."

"I do not want to stay in the army."

"Me, either," affirmed Johnny.

"Well, boys, we got to for a while yet," Jesse assured them. "Though the end is getting near. Are you aware of the general orders that are comin' down from the War Department?"

"Did you tell us about them?"

"Am now. There are a lot of units, a lot of men, already being mustered out. The B&O is bringin' tens of thousands of Sherman's fellows back. You know, the fellows who have served the longest. Anyway, general orders say that when we are discharged we get to keep our uniforms, knapsacks, haversacks, canteens. They're ours. And, boys, if yer so inclined, you can purchase your gun."

"Hmmm. What on God's earth would we do with a haversack?"

"Don't know about you, but I intend to pack my daily rations in it on the way to the shop each morning." Jesse flashed one of his now-expected playful grins. "I think I'll eat salt pork and hard bread every single day for the rest of my life."

"Are you gonna buy your gun, Corporal?"

"I'm hopin' to. I don't know how much it will cost us yet, but I hope to. My Colt. I'd like to have that."

They fell silent for a while. Other conversations distracted them. The heat of the day distracted them. Jesse knew they would be stopping soon at some appropriate spot. The horses needed water, and they all needed rest. He loosened his bandanna from around his neck and used it to wipe the sweat off his face. Drawing it across his growing mustache, he wondered again how his womenfolk would take to it.

Pretty snorted and tossed her head lightly. It was her way of telling Jesse that she needed attention. He patted her neck. "We'll be there soon, pretty lady."

*Don't fall in love with your horse, boys. They're just a tool. Like your firearm. They're replaceable. Don't think otherwise.* Somebody in training had spoken those words to the men. Jesse hadn't liked hearing it then and didn't like thinking on it now. "I wish I could take you with me, Pretty, but I can't. You understand that, don't you? I can't. I know I can't afford to buy you even if I wanted to. We've already got one horse for the shop. We can't have two."

"D'dya say somethin', Corporal?"

"Just thinkin' out loud, Johnny. Pay no mind." Jesse held a controlled look on his face but inside his heart was laid open.

**\*\*\*\***

He slid the saddle off Pretty's back, preparing to rub her down for the night and feed her. When they stopped, they'd been ordered to make camp. The ride was proving so uneventful there was no need to push themselves or the horses.

"I'm supposin' we don't need all seven days' rations," commented Danny. "We're going to get there early."

"You can risk it and eat hearty tonight," said Jesse. "They probably expected us not to need it all, unless we ran into trouble."

"Two servings of hard bread and jerky. Just what I want. Now if it was beef stew . . ."

Jesse's attention was drawn away from the horses—a woman's voice? He glanced in the direction it came from. A group of bedraggled civilians had approached a cluster of officers from the Ohio regiment. *Probably more refugees. Wonder what they want?* And then the voice again. Familiar. *What? Reminds me of someone.*

"Charley, will you tend to my girl?" He had to figure this out. "I'll much appreciate it." Charley, too, had noticed the civilian party and nodded his consent, curious as to what the corporal would find out.

Jesse sidled close enough to the ongoing conversation to attempt to hear without being obvious. It didn't work. When close enough to hear, he was close enough to be seen. The voice belonged to a girl, not a woman, and she was looking straight at him. "Jesse?" she gasped.

"My God, Effie."

The major, their commanding officer, spoke pointedly to Jesse. "Do you know these people, Corporal?"

Jesse was momentarily speechless; he was so taken aback. "Speak up, boy," the major continued. "You either do or you don't."

"Uh, yes, Sir." Jesse managed to stammer. "She's kin, Sir." He realized that he was nervously fiddling with the collar on his jacket. He stopped. Regaining control, he stood to attention and saluted. "Is there anything I can do, Sir?"

"Yes, Corporal . . . Corporal who?"

"Jesse J. Cook, Sir. 53rd Kentucky."

The major drummed his hand on his right leg. "Well, Corporal Cook, since you seem to know this young woman, take care of her and them." He waved his arm in a general arc that took in Effie and the four others with her. "They're hungry, I take it. Do what you can. We all have extra rations." And with that the officers resumed what they'd been doing.

Jesse walked tentatively towards Effie. He had no idea what to say to her. *And who are these people? Are they related to me?* A fellow about Jesse's age stood protectively near to Effie. He was scowling, eyes angry, his hand on Effie's shoulder. More than his posture, Jesse noticed the Confederate uniform—filthy, worn, with a sergeant's chevron, Virginia regiment. *Golderned, he outranks me.*

Behind them two women stared mostly at their feet. Now and then they sneaked furtive glances at the soldiers slowly gathering around.

There was one more, another veteran, a private by visible rank. He was an older fellow, limping. He showed no signs of rancor, but just looked exhausted, resigned, empty.

"I'm glad to see that you're . . . alive," said Jesse. He could not use the word *well,* for she looked far from that.

"And I'm pained to see that you been wounded."

Jesse nodded, well aware that his scar was still obvious. "Would you care to sit?" Effie and the others looked around, unsure where they might do that. Words failed Jesse then, and he felt unsure what to do next. The Reb sergeant just continued to glare at the Union soldiers, at Jesse, at Jesse's revolver slung on his hip.

*All right,* Jesse thought. *How in tarnation do I break through to this fellow?* He recalled their orders: *Behave as true soldiers, patriots, and gentlemen. Show the sergeant we mean no harm.* He unbuckled his belt and let his holster with the Colt slide off, handing it to Joe who was standing close by. Stepping towards the sergeant, Jesse extended his hand. The fellow balled a fist at his side.

"Jesse," Effie blurted. "This is my brother, Hiram Gentry. If'n I'm kin of yours, then so is he."

Hiram Gentry hissed, "I ain't kin to no Yankee."

Jesse refused to match the man's mindless anger. Part of him wanted to. *Someone like this filthy bastard, this so-called cousin, killed Pete.*

Drawing himself up, Jesse said stiffly, "Sergeant . . . Hiram." Then, turning to Effie, he urged. "Please, join us for dinner. We do have plenty. Like the Major said, we have more than we need. Army rations. Coffee." He gestured for her to pass in front of him towards the cooking fire that Johnny had brought to life.

Hiram roughly seized his sister's arm, halting her. "How do you know him?"

"He helped me once. Back home. Saved me."

"Saved you? He was at the home place? Effie, was he in the cabin?" Hiram raised his hand as if to strike her, but Jesse was quicker. He grabbed his cousin's arm and flung him to the ground, planting a boot firmly on his heaving chest.

"Mistreat this girl, and you're no better than the filthy scoundrels we scared off." As Hiram strained to roll free, Jesse bore down with his heel. "When I let you up, show us the Golderned *Virginia cavalier* that you're supposed to be." Firearm or no, Hiram knew who was in charge.

"Can you do that?" Jesse growled, raising his eyebrows just short of mockery. His cousin looked up at the soldiers all around him and nodded. Jesse removed his boot and stepped back. Hiram, unassisted, slowly got to his feet, brushing dirt from his rumpled coat. A pistol's ominous metallic *click!* froze him. Sergeant Blackwood, his Union counterpart, purred, "I suggest you accept the corporal's hospitality."

"Okay, yeah. . . . sure."

Blackwood slid his revolver back into the holster, turned and asked the platoon members to gather what rations they could spare. He would not order them, and neither did Jesse.

It did not take long, though, for a sufficient number of biscuits to be passed around, coffee to be brewed, and beans simmered with jerky. Jesse's squad members, who had met Effie in Virginia, were quick to offer what they had and fell into an easy camaraderie.

"Last time we sat like this was on the floor of your cabin," said Danny.

Effie smiled weakly. "I remember.  I was so cross."

"No matter," Danny replied. "You were scared."

"We had a good fire goin'," Johnny remembered. "Twas right nice."

Hiram sat beside his sister, gobbling down whatever food was offered, saying nothing.

"Your grandfather?" Jesse asked. "Did he . . ."

"Yes," whispered Effie. "He passed—in January. The winter was too hard. You were right about that."

"I'm sorry. I wish my Ma could maybe have spoken to him some day. She told me she had kin in those mountains.  I would've liked her and your grandpa to talk about that."

Hiram swallowed, then spat on the ground. "Which one of yous knocked him down to begin with? It was yous, wasn't it? A defenseless old man. Damn

Yankees. Effie told me somethin' happened back in December. Never said exactly what."

"Hiram, stop," Effie scolded. "You don't know what you're talkin' about. I never told you the whole story 'cause I didn't want to get you riled. Or think unkindly of me." She swallowed, shaken. "Grandpa tried to kill Jesse with a pick ax. You know how ornery he could be. He didn't know how Jesse had come along and saved me from being . . ."

Jesse interrupted her. "You don't have to talk about this—not for my benefit."

But she continued. "When Grandpa kept coming at them, spooking their horses, waving that ax, the other soldier, Pete, just . . ." Suddenly quiet, she looked nervously around. "Where is Pete?"

She knew the answer from Jesse's expression before he uttered the words. "He was killed. In Virginia."

Effie gave a strangled cry and reached out to touch Jesse's sleeve. "I'm so sorry. And you were shot there, too. Weren't you? In my country."

Hiram cleared his throat. "Where at in Virginia?"

"Marion—near Saltville."

"I wasn't there."

"I didn't think so."

"Sergeant," said Blackwood, wanting to defuse the tension, "Where did you serve? Exactly? Were you with Lee?"

"I was . . . all the way to Appomattox."

"And him?" Blackwood jerked his head in the direction of the Confederate private.

"One o' my men. I'm lookin' after 'im. He's got no one else."

Joe let out a long whistle. They were sitting with veterans of the Army of Northern Virginia. Fabled warriors, these men.

Jesse looked at Hiram. "I like to think that under other circumstances you and I could have been friends, like cousins." He held up his hands, palms forward. "I'll never agree with the choices you made, but I admire you doin' what you felt you had to."

"Same." Hiram sat up straighter and took a breath. "It sounds like you was most kind to my sister. I reckon I'm indebted to ya. All of ya."

One of the older women began to cry. Joe took a blanket from his pack and draped it around her shoulders. She did not speak.

"Who are these women?" Jesse asked.

"They just took up with us," said Effie. "They don't talk much. Suffered a lot, I expect. Somethin' we said must have sparked a memory."

"We've all suffered—too much," said Jesse. "So, now, where ya goin'?"

"Covington."

"Really? Covington?"

"You said refugees were welcome there. That your Ma was there—named Gentry," Effie hurriedly explained.

"She is, and they are." Jesse grinned. "So, you're taking my advice."

"Maybe," Hiram said. "Somethin' else might come up. There's lots o' towns between here and Covington. I seen the map."

Danny leaned in towards Hiram. "Kentucky is full, crawlin' with, Southern vets and sympathizers. You'll find a place if you want it . . . But I would go to Covington. Jesse's folks'll help you."

"And my Ma is not the only Gentry. Her brother Valentine is there." He scrambled to his feet, returning with pen and paper. "Do you read?"

"I can," said Hiram. "Not Effie."

"Well, take this." Jesse wrote his parents' address, Valentine's address, and an introductory note. He handed it to Hiram, "And don't make me wish I hadn't told you where they live."

"You can trust us," said Effie. "Hiram?"

"Yeah. You can—a Gentry's honor." He clambered stiffly to his feet and gave Effie a hand. "We best be goin'."

"All right," said Jesse. He shoved his hands into his trousers pockets. The ragged band began to move away. Jesse watched them, his emotions torn.

"Wait," he yelled. "Effie . . . Hiram."

Effie turned to look at him, tears filling her eyes. "Oh, Jesse." She ran back to him and threw her arms around him. "Thank you."

"None of that," he said, taking his bandanna to dry her eyes. "Here. Hiram, take this. I don't have much, but you will need it more than I do." Jesse handed a fistful of coins and script to his cousin. "I'll get paid again sometime," he grinned. "And blankets. You should have blankets."

257

"Joe already gave us one."

"Well here's another," said Danny. "And a little more money . . ."

"Have some more tasty army rations," offered Johnny, holding out what he had.

Hiram gazed at them in astonishment. "Damn Yankees. How'm I supposed to hate you?" He managed a small crooked smile as he accepted the gifts, handing them off to the others in his group. The money he pocketed.

"I guess it's time to stop hating," said Jesse. He offered his hand. This time, Hiram took it.

"Corporal," Hiram said. "I hope you really are my cousin." He squared his shoulders, standing as straight and dignified as was possible under the circumstances. He looked into the faces of the Union soldiers, and then directly at Jesse. He saluted. Then motioning for the others to follow him, he moved away.

Jesse watched until the travelers were mere specks on the horizon. Joe stood with him. "I hope they find somewhere safe," he said.

"Me, too, Joe. Me, too."

# PART FIVE

## EVERY FOOT
## OF AMERICAN SOIL

# CHAPTER 33

**Covington, Kentucky**
**July 1865**

"Never thought I'd come here again." Riley gently touched his son's shoulder before sitting on the chair next to the hospital bed. He unconsciously began twisting his cap. "You don't look well, Son. Peaked. How do ya feel?"

Jesse grunted, attempted a smile. "Like shit, Pa." What he felt was feverish—still—his cheeks burning.

"I talked to the doctor. Internals. He told me it could've been somethin' you ate or somethin' you drank. Probably not your wound."

"Pa, how could getting shot in the head affect my gut? Oh, God, I just want to. . ."

"Sleep? Maybe I should go." Riley felt bad making Jesse even try to converse.

"No, Pa. Stay." Jesse blinked, shook his head as if trying to clear it, and pulled himself into a semisitting position. His father immediately sprang up to help him, repositioning the pillow behind his head.

"You're feverish."

"Hope that's not what I have, the fever."

"You don't, Son. They woulda had you quarantined. Your body's just fightin' whatever's inside makin' you ill. Good food and drink's what you need.

"No," moaned Jesse. "I never wanna eat again."

"I'll remember that when yer out o' here and your Ma or Eliza lays out a spread." Noticing the cup of water sitting on the table, Riley tentatively handed it to Jesse, "Don't throw it at me."

"Tastes bad," said Jesse, taking a sip.

"That's just you, Son. It'll pass. Before I forget, Martha's bringin' Eliza tomorrow . . . That is, if you want to see her."

"Course I do." Jesse's voice was soft, tired.

"Don't expect to have much time alone, if any. Martha's not likely to leave her."

Jesse managed a wry smile. "Alone, Pa? In here?"

Riley glanced down the hospital ward. "Suppose yer right, but you can at least drink in her sweet smell."

"Pa!"

"What? Can't I appreciate a comely miss? I'm not *that* old."

"Just not *my* miss," replied Jesse.

Riley chuckled. "I wouldn't stand a chance against you . . . Catherine, er, your Ma, will come with Eliza tomorrow. That will be even worse for you. All those women fussin'."

"It's fine."

"Your Ma will bring something to feed you whether you want to eat or not. And Martha will no doubt have some potion. But you know what, Jess? That woman knows things. Whatever she gives you for your gut, take. She's probably better at medicine than these doctors."

Jesse closed his eyes. He didn't want his father to leave. *I'm just so weak,* he thought. *Don't feel much like talking.* He was glad to be away from the camp, even under these circumstances. Daily life in the army had become so routine since their brief stint at the Gap, so non-eventful as to become boring. The 53$^{rd}$ had been sent back to Northern Kentucky to wait out their enlistment. They were so close to their homes, yet not home. The days dragged. Passes to leave camp had been non-existent—the need to maintain readiness. *Readiness? For what?*

"Penny for your thoughts," said Riley. He knew Jesse was not sleeping.

"Ain't worth a penny. Tell me the news, Pa . . . What's been goin' on? Just, don't make me *talk.*"

"I don't know how much you've been gettin' from the papers. Tens of thousands of soldiers 've been comin' through town, goin' one place or another to muster out and return home. The ones from the East, they've been comin' by steamer from Parkersburg. The Government is still impressin' boats and crews into service against their will."

Jesse's thoughts wandered, his eyes closed, as his father talked of low river levels, steamers run aground near Covington, steamers stuck at the Cincinnati landing, and literally hordes of men disembarking to loiter on the riverfront in hopes of soon moving on. Military guards had to be posted to protect all the cargo on the Public Landing. Soldiers had stolen casks of bacon and crates of whiskey. Nobody turned them in to authorities. In his mind, he was back on another riverboat, ice smashing at the hull.

"There've been a lot of former Rebs in town," continued Riley. "And fights have broken out over and over. Do you remember our former city marshal James Wentworth? He got into it with Frank Estep at the Clinton House on Madison Avenue. Frank's brother Tom is a former Rebel officer, and Frank apparently is at the very least *sympathizin'*. The short of it is that Frank drew a revolver on Wentworth, fired but missed, and then one of the Esteps hit him on the head with a mug. Both Esteps were arrested."

"I've heard those names. Can't recollect meeting them," said Jesse.

"I thought you weren't going to talk," chided Riley.

"What else? Go on."

"Let me think. There's been a number of famous generals and folks goin' through town, mostly Cincinnati side. Sherman and his wife. Custer. Burnside, and the wife of Confederate General Breckinridge."

Jesse flinched. Suddenly agitated. Riley reached out to him again. "What'd I say, Son? What's wrong?"

Jesse looked at his father, tears pooling in his already rheumy eyes. "Breckinridge was in command when this happened." He slowly ran his hand over his scars, down his cheek. "When Pete died. . ." Raw emotion contorted his face. "Did they put out the *red carpet* for her?"

"I believe she had the permission of President Johnson to pass through, yes, but no celebrations."

Jesse sank into his thoughts. *It's time to stop hating.* He remembered his own words, thought of Hiram and Effie. "Pa," he whispered, "Any news about people we know?"

"Sure is. I was plannin' on tellin' you. My brother Frank is home. His unit was discharged and brought back from New Orleans."

"Uncle Frank . . . How is he?"

"Not good, I'm afraid. He looks about like you, but is tryin' not to show it. He's back workin' with me for now."

"What happened?"

"He was in the hospital down there. Was released just 'fore the whole lot of them came North. He did have the fever, Jess. It didn't kill 'im, but it seems to have ruined him."

"Sorry to hear that, Pa."

"John Hunt Morgan," continued Riley. "A number of his men have been returning. Some o' them are back livin' in Covington and Newport. Others just passin' through." He paused to gauge

Jesse's reaction. "Maybe you don't wanna hear about those guerrillas."

"Just one," muttered Jesse. "Eliza has a cousin."

"Name's Marion Allender," replied Riley. "He's been seen."

"I guess she'll be glad . . . Kin's kin in the end."

Riley looked hard at his son. "This war was one hell of a mess. Whether you were in it, like you, or here, like me . . . Never knowin' who the enemy was. Friends fightin' friends. Cousins enlisting on opposing sides. Golderned, Jess, our forefathers knew who the enemy was—the British, Mexicans." Standing he brushed the now-longish hair from his son's eyes. "I am going to let you rest now. You need it."

"Just one more thing, Pa. Have any refugees showed up at the house? Any Gentrys?"

"Not that I ever heard. And yer Ma's been workin' some with that group, the Ladie's Refugee Relief Commission. Why, Son?"

"No matter, Pa. I was just hopin'—wonderin'."

Riley nodded and moved to depart. He knew Jesse would confide in time if he felt the need. He watched his son slump into a posture ripe for sleep. "Before you doze off . . . I like your mustache. You wear it well." He wasn't sure that he was even heard.

# CHAPTER 34

**Mid-September 1865**

The train rattled and creaked, heading Northeast, tracks hugging the Ohio. Not a great distance—Louisville to Covington, a hundred miles give or take. Jesse stared out the window, gazing at the river when it came into view, drops of rain making dirty pathways cross the glass. *This is it, then,* he thought. *No longer a soldier.* He moved his thumbs over the discharge papers held in his hands, not looking at them. He had read them to distraction—honorably discharged.

He sat alone, having thrown his gear in the seat next to him. He just didn't want to talk about it. It was exactly one year and two days since he had enlisted. *Three hundred and sixty-seven days. So much has happened. Honorably discharged.* Slowly, he folded the paper into a smaller rectangle and jammed it in his jacket pocket.

It was strange how the Army worked, stationed one place, sent totally somewhere else to muster out. They had ridden to Louisville, turned their horses in to the Quartermaster there. Then the rest of it: collecting final pay, settling accounts, signing papers, listening to encouraging words from the regimental officers. Hugs and backslaps all round. Kentucky bourbon.

The worst had been leaving Pretty. He had felt like bawling. Through sheer force of will, though, he managed to show no emotion at all. He led her to a stall, took off her tack, patted her down, and saw to her feed. She seemed to sense that he would never return. Perhaps it was in his touch. *Or was that my imagination?* He had sprinted from that stable, not daring to look back. *Someone will buy her, surely. She's a good horse, strong, still spirited.* He understood that many of their horses—some said most—would be headed for the slaughterhouse. *Not her. Please, God, not Pretty.*

The train swayed as it rounded a bend in the river. Jesse's hand slid from the armrest, brushing the holster of his revolver as it did so. He allowed his fingers to caress the familiar leather, now worn smooth. He had purchased the Colt. He wasn't sure why he wanted it so badly; he just did. They had deducted its cost from his pay, which was all right. The half of his bonus kept safe by Uncle Henry awaited him at home. He'd be okay for a while. *We'll most likely live with Pa after we're married. Just have to pay for our keep. Someday . . . a house of my own. Or a bigger house for all of us . . . A bigger shop.*

Sergeant Blackwood interrupted Jesse's reverie. He nodded towards the seat. "Mind if I sit?"

"No, 'course not." With one swoop of his arm, Jesse cleared the seat of gear, shoving it to the floor, then proceeded to kick it under the seat in front of him.

"I couldn't part with mine, either," Blackwood chuckled. "Seems we've grown attached to our side arms." The sergeant could not help but notice Jesse's mood. "This is a difficult day. I never expected it to be."

"Yeah, Sarge, it is."

"When are you going to call me by my given name?"

Jesse smiled. "It just never seemed right."

"Well, we're civilians now. Use it."

"Okay, Robert."

"Bob, not Robert. What're you plannin' on doing with yours?"

"My what? The Colt?"

"Yeah, your pistol."

"Polish it—endlessly."

Bob let out an audible laugh. "We're certainly practiced."

"I just figured I'd keep it somewhere safe but handy. Just in case. And, who knows, they may form a militia. I'll join up if they do."

"Didn't get enough of the Army?" replied Bob. "If you're serious, hold out for a commission."

"An officer?"

"At least a First Sergeant. You're good enough. Yer record sparkles."

"Thanks. You goin' back to the store?"

"It's family. Don't have much choice. Unless I wanna go with Stu."

"Stu? What about 'im?"

"He wants to go West. Might even join the cavalry out there."

"Tarnation. I did not know that. He wants to fight Indians? Not me."

"You got a future, Jess. Eliza. Your shop. Stu doesn't. And he's a damn good soldier. They'll take him if he chooses to enlist."

"It's all so troublin', Sarge . . . Bob. I feel like I'm being torn apart. I wanna go home. Of course, I wanna go home, but . . . It's like I'm losin' family members. Tarnation. Why is this so hard?"

Bob punched Jesse playfully on the shoulder. "Those of us in town just gotta make a pact to keep in touch. Invite me to your wedding. Invite all of us. We'll take you out to some saloon and try to talk you out of it."

Jesse grinned. "You can get me tight. I'd enjoy that. But you'll never talk me out of it. Wait 'til you see Liza."

Danny and Charley came stumbling down the aisle. "Never could walk on a damn train," laughed Danny.

"Have you been at the bottle again?" teased Jesse.

"Charley," Danny said mischievously, "Look at them. Our corporal. Our sergeant. We don't have to listen to them anymore. Not about drinkin'. Not about nothin'."

"Shut it," replied Jesse. "You'll always listen to me. It's second nature to you."

"Ha."

"We were just talkin' about you boys," said Bob. "How we're gonna miss ya. God knows why . . . But we will. We all gotta stay in touch . . . Oh, and call me Bob."

"Bob?"

"I do have a given name, Charley."

"I don't know if I can. It's just . . . you're the sergeant."

"Maybe once he takes off his Colt," said Jesse, "You'll feel more comfortable. Or, just call him Sarge when you see him 'round town. He'll prob'ly answer."

Blackwood smiled, "I think I would."

\*\*\*\*

When the train pulled in it was over—the 53rd scattered. Young men bound together in camaraderie were now hungry for home and hearth. Few were met by anyone. That would have required a telegram. Most preferred to be the surprise at the door, the knock that would be remembered for a lifetime. Some of the officers hailed a hack. The enlisted chose to walk, as Jesse did—as far as the market.

"I'm splittin' off here, Bob." He jerked his head in the direction he intended to go. "I wanna go down by the river."

"The river? What for? Thought your shop was that way." He motioned in the opposite direction.

"It is. I just need to go to the river. It's pretty as the sun sets. Need to think."

"Just be careful, Jess. There's no doubt bad eggs down there. Hit you on the head and rob you in a heartbeat."

"I'm still armed."

"Yep, guess we're still soldiers—at heart." Jesse began to move away. A look of concern crossed Blackwood's face. "Corporal." He shook his head. "I suppose I'll always call you that, but . . . whatever it is, *Jesse*, don't think on it too much. You done good. You done real good."

"Thanks, *Sarge*." Jesse smiled and extended his hand. "So, did you."

The huge tower of the great bridge came into view long before he reached the riverfront. It stood tall but desolate. Almost forlorn. No progress had been made on its construction since work was suspended during the war.

*Wish you were here, Pete. God, how I wish you were here.* Jesse gazed up at the skeleton of the unfinished bridge before moving down to the river's edge. *Now that men are returning . . . Jobs . . . I hope there'll be money to start again.*

It had been a little over a year, that's all, since he first met Pete—here at this very spot. What a night they'd had, drinking and collaring criminals. What an immediate bond they had formed. Like brothers. Best of chums.

Jesse picked up a stone and set it skimming across the water. *It's over, Pete. We got discharged today, and most of us returned home whole. At least, we appear 'whole'. There's big chunks of our insides that are still raw, bleeding. I hated leaving you there—in Virginia . . . So sorry I couldn't lead you cross that field . . . So very sorry.* He slumped down onto the ground, his shoulders hunched, his head bowed. His hat slid off his head, landing near his clenched fists. He did not hear the footsteps.

"Hey, mister. You drunk?"

Jesse instinctively whipped out his revolver and swung his body in the direction of the speaker, ending up prone, ready to fire. He faced two males, faces shadowed in the twilight. *Boys. They're just boys. Younger than Theo even.*

"Jimminy!" yelled the shorter of the two, stepping back.

"You plannin' on robbin' me?" purred Jesse.

"Was . . . ain't now."

"Get outta here." The taller boy skedaddled at top speed. His accomplice, though, stayed put. "Why aren't you leavin'?"

"Yer a soldier. Union. I never almost-robbed a soldier." The boy started moving towards Jesse, his face now visible. He seemed excited, awe-struck. "Did you kill any Rebs?"

"Jesus," said Jesse, clambering to his feet and holstering his Colt. "Are you outta your mind? How old are you? Aren't you supposed to be home? What's your name?"

The boy grinned. "That's a lot of questions. Are you a sergeant? Were you the boss?"

"Never was a sergeant. These are a corporal's stripes. You should learn that." He bent down to retrieve his hat before it found its way into the river. The boy eyed that, too.

"How many people have you robbed?" demanded Jesse.

"One . . . sort of. None."

"How can you *sort of* rob somebody?"

"He was drunk, so, we just hepped ourselfs to his stuff."

"Well, I'm not drunk and I suggest you get a new line of work before somebody does shoot you. Now get outta here and leave me alone."

The boy still didn't leave. When Jesse began to walk closer to the bridge the boy followed him. "Corporal. Corporal!" he hollered.

Jesse spun around. "What in tarnation! Don't call me that. I'm not a soldier anymore. War's over."

"Ya look like a soldier. What are ya, then?"

"Before the war, I was a cooper. I'll do that again." Jesse smiled. This boy so reminded him of his younger brothers, so in awe of all things military, all things grown-up. "Whatever your name is, do you know what a *cooper* is?"

"Makes barrels. You think I'm stupid?"

Jesse's mind flashed back to the night he met Pete, when practically the same words came out of his mouth. "Nah, I know yer not stupid." Impulsively, Jesse took his Hardee hat and pressed it on the boy's head. "Here, you wear it, as a souvenir. I won't need this makin' barrels."

"Bully!" The boy's grin lit up his face, exposing missing front teeth. Then as if to avoid the possibility that this soldier might change his mind and shoot him after all, he spun and darted off.

Jesse let out a belly laugh, calling after him. "Wear it proud, bub. And go home."


"That boy reminds me of you, Strong. Same hard-case attitude. Never did tell me his name. Prob'ly kin of yours." Jesse realized that he was speaking out loud. He glanced around. No one to hear him.

A boat's whistle pierced the moment. Looking again towards the river, he watched a steamboat pushing back from the public landing on the opposite—Ohio—shore. He admired the huge paddlewheel, which was kicking up mud from the river bottom as it churned mightily, laboriously propelling the boat to the shipping channel, where the engineer would thrust the engines into a forward gear. "What a thing of beauty. Raw power."

Once more he raised his eyes to the great bridge. "Just like this bridge." For an instant, he thought he caught a glimpse of Pete, pulling on a line, as one with the bridge as he had been with his horse, his carbine, but it was just a trick of the mind. The play of setting sun and shadows on the water.

*I came down here hoping to say good-bye to you, Pete. I've got to sort through this. Somehow.*

*Move on. Somehow. The captain told us to show as much grit every day rebuilding this country as we showed on the field of battle. Is that what we're supposed to do now? Rebuild our country? That's a tough order. Tarnation, wasn't winning the war enough? Isn't caring for one's family enough?*

He ambled back to where he'd been sitting, bent to pick up his gear, and paused to gaze once more at the river. He listened to it, the never-ending lapping at the shore as it coursed westward, always on the move. He swung his gear onto his shoulder. It was almost dark.

With a long sigh, Jesse thought again of the boy. Thought of his own younger brothers. Said aloud, "Maybe the captain was right, Pete. Maybe the job's not finished. And what've we got to lose in tryin'? We've already done the hard part." Pivoting on the well-worn boots that had carried him so far, he turned towards home. It was a short three-block walk. Without conscious thought he began to whistle.

General Orders No. 108
To: Soldiers of the Armies of the United States
From: General Ulysses S. Grant

By your patriotic devotion to your country in the hour
of danger and alarm—your magnificent fighting, bravery, and
endurance—you have maintained the supremacy of the Union
and the Constitution, overthrown all armed opposition to the
enforcement of the laws, and of the proclamation forever
abolishing slavery—the cause and pretext of the rebellion—and
opened the way to the rightful authorities to restore order and
inaugurate peace on a permanent and enduring basis on every
foot of American soil. . . .

# About Jesse

*Jesse J. Cook — two portraits*

*Left: circa 1880s; Jesse in his late thirties*
*Right: circa 1900; Jesse in his mid-fifties.*

## The Basics: Cook Family Genealogy

In 1861, when President Abraham Lincoln called for men to uphold the Constitution of the United States by enlisting in the Union Army, Jesse Cook was barely sixteen years old. By the time the conflict was over, he was a twenty-year-old veteran. Like many a young man, he came of age during what could arguably be termed the most tumultuous years in American history.

Jesse's father, Joseph Riley Cook, was pardoned and released from Joliet Prison in Illinois at the same time that the first troops were being organized into fighting units. By that time, Riley had already served about 18 months of a three-year sentence for burglary. There are no known records showing why he was pardoned. Two men imprisoned with him were not. What is known, is that his oldest son—Jesse—would have been the "man of the house" at 14-15 years of age, with a mother and three younger brothers, experiencing whatever hardship that would have entailed.

J. Riley Cook was one of three sons born to Henry S. Cook and Lydia Ramsey about 1822. His older brother was Benjamin Franklin Cook, who did serve in the Civil War during the same period as

Jesse, despite being a man in his forties. Riley did not enlist, nor did his brother Henry.

Jesse is descended from Scottish and English ancestry and a long line of soldier patriots. His mother was Catherine Gentry. The Gentrys were a Colonial family of English descent, who settled throughout Virginia and the Carolinas, eventually migrating throughout the South. Jesse's paternal family, the Cooks, were originally called MacCook (according to family lore). The prefix was dropped in the Colonial era. Jesse's grandfather, Henry S. Cook, was from New York and may have served in the artillery in the War of 1812. The Ramseys are also of Scottish descent. Jesse's 2$^{nd}$ Great-Grandfather Giles Ramsey was a gunner on a privateer named the "Fire Brand" that sailed out of Philadelphia to prey on British merchant shipping and smugglers during the American Revolution. Another of Jesse's ancestors was probably captain and owner of the ship. A great uncle (also named Giles Ramsey) fought and died during the War of 1812, serving with General Andrew Jackson at the Battle of New Orleans.

The three Cook brothers were all trained as coopers, which is the art of making wooden barrels of every size and description. Up until the early 20$^{th}$ Century, barrels and kegs were used to store virtually everything, dry or liquid. It was a trade which would afford a man a secure living. Riley passed on his skills to his sons, as would Jesse to his.

Jesse was the oldest of five boys. He was born in 1845. His younger brothers were Andrew Jackson

Cook, born 1849; Theodore Parker Cook (Theo), born 1851; James Valentine Cook (Jimmy/Jimbo), born 1858; and William Ellsworth Cook (the toddler in our story), born 1862. All lived to adulthood except for Andy, who apparently died before the war began.

## Jesse and Eliza—A Family

It didn't take Jesse long to marry his "comely miss." He was discharged from the army in mid-September of 1865. He and Eliza married in her hometown of Ripley, Ohio, six months later, on March 13, 1866. Jesse was just shy of his twenty-first birthday. Eliza was seventeen.

Jesse and Eliza's first recorded birth of a child is that of Martha Jane Cook, born in 1870. This baby would have been named after Eliza's mother and grandmother. Baby Martha lived at least five months, but died sometime during infancy. Given the fact that Jesse and Eliza married in 1866, it is likely that another child was born and died previous to Martha. The couple would lose at least two more children in their lifetime, one child living to age ten before passing. There was no shortage of heartache.

However, there was also a procession of healthy Cook children who grew to adulthood. Most of them were girls. Jesse's one and only son was born six years after he and Eliza were wed. Joseph Riley Cook (named after Jesse's father) came into the world in 1872. One can only imagine Jesse's joy at conceiving a son, someone to follow in his coopering footsteps. Over the next twenty years, Eliza would bear five daughters who survived and two other children who did not. Jesse's girls were Carrie, Stella, Lyda, Grace, and Effie. Jesse's youngest daughter, born when he was 49 years old, was named for his grandmother Effie Gentry.

## Jesse's Early Years as a Cooper

Jesse and Eliza did reside with Riley for some years after the war, but by the time Jesse was thirty, and the father of two children, he had his family out on their own in Covington. The cooper shop was located at the southwest corner of East Park St. and Stewart Alley. Jesse moved his young family away from the site of the cooper shop, to what was probably a more residential area. They rented the rear section of a house at 324 Greenup St., about two to three blocks distant.

Something substantial occurred between Jesse and his father by 1877. Jesse was thirty-two. Riley was still very much a vital man at fifty-five. He would work as a cooper for many more years, but never again with Jesse. What appeared to be a partnership disintegrated by '77. The name of the cooperage changed. It was now *J.J. Cook Cooperage Manufactury*. The new sign would seem to indicate that Jesse was achieving his dream. Theo was working with Jesse and fifteen-year-old Willie was probably his apprentice. But Jesse's control of the business was short-lived. By 1879 he pulled up stakes and left Covington, leaving behind his livelihood, his father and brothers. His mother, Catherine, had died by 1872.

What prompted Jesse's apparent estrangement from his father may have been very personal, not business-related. A woman by the name of Eliza Young Gentry had been living with Jesse's family for some years. She was divorced from Catherine's brother Valentine. Riley must have married his sister-in-law very shortly after Martha died. In 1873, Eliza and Riley gave birth to a son. By the time Jesse left town there were two more new little Cooks. These half-brothers and sisters were the same age as Jesse and Eliza's children.

Perhaps it was just too much—too many mouths to feed—for one shop to sustain. That seems unlikely motivation, though, to leave town. Large families were the norm, and Covington was a booming city in 1877. There would have been other work for an experienced cooper with Jesse's skills. He obviously felt compelled to leave, completely leave, but why?

What was Jesse running from? Business conflicts with his father? Or something more personal, an animosity caused by his father's remarriage and second family? Whatever the reason, Jesse appeared to be troubled. He sought spiritual guidance, joining the Union Methodist Episcopal Church and dragging his young brother William with him. In September of 1878 he was received as a full member of said church, but by April of 1879 he was removed from the rolls. Jesse was gone.

He moved to Pendleton County, Kentucky, whose largest town of Falmouth sits on the Licking River, a tributary of the Ohio. Pendleton County was a long-time residence of many in the Allender family, first cousins of Jesse's Eliza. Another of Eliza's cousins was Frank Stallcup. Frank was only slightly older than Jesse, and also a cooper by trade. He shared Jesse's experience as a horse soldier in the Union Army, and he lived and worked in Falmouth. It would have been the natural place for this young family to go in an attempt to start over . . . Eliza bore her daughter Stella while in Pendleton County. Jesse was on the tax rolls, but it does not appear that he ever opened a shop of his own.

It is important to note, that when Jesse decided to leave Cook's Cooperage, he did not completely abandon his brothers. In fact, he may have assumed a role as head of his family, while his father concentrated on raising a second. In 1881, it was Jesse, not Riley, who provided "supporting facts" and signed for then 18-year-old William E. Cook to obtain a marriage license. There is compelling evidence to suggest that Jesse took Willie with him when he relocated to Falmouth.

By 1885 Pendleton County was not offering what Jesse needed. He returned to Covington around this time, never to work as a cooper in Kentucky again. He would reside in Covington, but he set his sights on working for the large, booming cooperages across the river in Cincinnati—the giant manufacturing firms that he had only dreamed of. Innovations in industry were transforming the ancient trade of cooperage. With the healing of the bonds between North and South, the American Industrial Revolution was climbing towards its zenith.

## Jesse's Wound—the Pension Papers

Coincident with the post-war industrial boom, America's two million veterans were feeling their age. By 1890, when the Dependent Pension Act was passed by Congress, the nation's veterans were mostly in their 40's and 50's. Most were dependent upon manual labor at some level to support themselves and their families. They had survived the war outwardly intact, but many were physically and emotionally damaged by what they had endured. Given that it was growing more difficult for these men to maintain working at a high-level of physical labor, they demanded a relaxation of the pension laws. They demanded assistance from their government. The political pressure on Congress was intense. Under previous law, veterans were compensated for grievous wounds, and widows and children of men killed or mortally wounded were compensated. With this new legislation of 1890, men could be granted a pension based on a disability that was not directly a result of the war. In time, old age itself would be considered a disability.

The nation had decided to honor its veterans with economic assistance. Jesse was one of these veterans when he traveled to Louisville at 45 years of age to apply.

When Jesse was mustered out of the army, his records stated that he had suffered a "gunshot wound in head." The medical records are not clear as to whether a bullet actually lodged in his head, or if it was a grazing wound. An obvious scar, though, is still visible on Jesse's portrait taken in the 1890s. His hair never regrew on that part of his scalp. The doctors diagnosed Jesse with "naso-pharyngeal catarrh and total deafness of right ear." That was the ear below his wound. They concluded that he had a "partial inability to earn support by manual labor." He was awarded a pension, which was increased within a few years. Also noted at the time of Jesse's medical review was that he suffered from a digestive disorder and piles. He could probably argue that both of those maladies arose from his time in a mounted force, enduring unsanitary conditions.

## Jesse's Later Years as a Cooper

Jesse worked throughout the 1890's at the sprawling VanAgthoven's Cooperage on W. Front St. in Cincinnati. By the end of that decade he had worked through the ranks and was offered the position of foreman, which he held for fourteen years—until his death. Both his brother Theo and his son, Joe, worked with him (or for him) at various times at VanAgthoven's.

In those days, foremen were known for being hard-nosed, tough, unforgiving, sometimes despised by the workmen. They were the men who kept a factory operating. They managed the men who managed the machines and wielded the tools. They were the link between the supervisors and owners and the workmen. Jesse J. Cook, the non-com in the army, found himself doing basically the same thing on the factory floor: executing orders to achieve an objective, maximizing results while minimizing disruption, greasing the cogs of industry for a nation on the rise.

There is no way of knowing what kind of foreman Jesse was, how he maintained charge of his departments. We must assume, however, that as far as management is concerned, he was very successful. They would not have employed him for so many years had his units not produced. It is not presumptuous to state that Jesse was probably demanding but fair. In the end, workers usually reflect the treatment they receive. Productive departments would suggest an effective foreman.

## And Some Fascinating Facts

Searching through genealogical records and old newspapers can provide some tantalizing insights into the mindset of a time in history, of the characters of the people one is researching. Family oral history and studying old photographs can do likewise. I want to share a few which influenced the telling of this story, and others which are just interesting.

<u>Eliza</u>:

As an old woman Eliza was known in her family for being the Grandma who made potions and balms. It was easy to progress from that knowledge to making her mother Martha a folk-healer with pioneer skills in the use of herbs and plants.

Eliza was very close to her family, a large cadre of cousins. After Jesse's death, Eliza survived another twelve years. A year after Jesse's death, she remarried. She married her first cousin, John W. Allender, an engineer. (They were next door neighbors growing up.) The two married in their hometown of Ripley, Ohio, but lived in Covington. Eliza is buried with William Allender. Her grave stone gives no indication that Jesse ever existed in her life.

Eliza attempted to fraud the federal government. In 1913, a war widow who remarried was no longer eligible to collect the veteran's pension. But Eliza did not inform the Bureau of Pensions of her marriage to Allender. It is not known if this was through ignorance, oversight, or purposeful. One expects it was intentional, for one of her daughters, Grace Elvira Cook, wrote to the Bureau and ratted on her. She asserted that Eliza J. Cook, a pensioner as widow of Jesse J. Cook, had "been married for a few months past to one John Allender." An investigation followed and Eliza lost—no more pension. There were no legal ramifications.

Why would a daughter report her mother in a situation such as this unless she were angry, at the remarriage itself, or a perceived affront to a beloved father?

Riley:

Not much is known about Riley's later life. At some point he joined the Mason's. He is buried in the Masonic Lodge section of Highland Cemetery in Ft. Mitchell, Kentucky, just south of Covington. His second wife is buried next to him. They have simple headstones. Riley's bears the Masonic emblem. The details of Catherine's death and burial seem lost to history. Riley's brother, Henry, has a huge family plot with a towering obelisk in Highland. It is an easy walk from Riley's resting place.

Joe (Jesse's only son):

Jesse trained his son as a cooper, and young Joe worked in that trade into the 20th Century. At one point, he, too, was a foreman, but not at Van Agthoven's. I find it interesting that he followed so closely in his father's footsteps at a young age. Joe lived through the collapse of cooperage as a viable trade. The 20th Century saw the birth of new container choices: boxes and crates made of wood and cardboard, wooden barrels morphing into corrugated and steel drums. A need for wine barrels, beer kegs, and other niche barrels would remain, but the large cooperages would die. Joe progressed through a series of jobs—no real career.

<u>The Military</u>:

Jesse enlisted as a private in the 53<sup>rd</sup> Volunteer Mounted Infantry in September of 1864. Within ten days he was promoted to a non-com rank of corporal, earning the right to wear those two stripes on his arm. Privates in those days wore no stripe at all. Obviously, this young man of nineteen impressed someone with his mindset and/or leadership ability.

There was a militia recorded in Covington/Kenton County, Kentucky, after the war. It was probably like the pre-war militias, basically a unit on paper, with no enlisting or military activity of note. Jesse, Theo, and Riley are listed as members of the militia (as are every able-bodied man of age in that community). There may have been named officers. There were probably few, if any, gatherings of this group, much less drill. Many pre-war militias, if they did meet, found it an excuse to drink and carouse.

When Jesse applied for his pension there was a list of applicants from the area where he resided at the time. Of the ten or so men on the list, Jesse was the only one who arrived with medical papers and documentation in hand. That's a definite insight into his personality. Directly below Jesse's entry is one of a fellow member of the 53<sup>rd</sup>. This man, and I'm sure Jesse must have known him since they served in the same regiment and lived near each other, was disabled due to a fall from his horse. There were many dangers and mishaps which confronted those soldiers. In Jesse's regiment, one officer and eight enlisted men were killed and mortally wounded during the war. Forty enlisted men died of disease. It is not recorded how many like Jesse suffered a gunshot wound and recovered.

## Jesse's Death

Jesse died on February 9, 1913, at his home on Philadelphia St. in Covington. The house is still standing as of this writing, a three-story brick townhouse typical of the city—substantive but plain. The official cause of death was a cerebral hemorrhage or paralysis, what we would call a stroke. It is not known how long he may have lingered before he died, but not too long. According to the Cincinnati City Directory he was employed at VanAgthoven's Cooperage as a foreman cooper in 1912.

He was 67 years old at the time of his death.

Jesse's obituary simply states: *Jesse Cook, 67, formerly in the cooperage business, died yesterday at his home . . . He was a veteran of the Civil War, and leaves a widow and several grown children.*

One of those grown children was my grandmother, who must have loved him dearly. Her only request of her daughter in later years was to be taken to her Papa's grave to maintain it and lay flowers.

Jesse is buried in the Civil War section of Covington's Linden Grove Cemetery. He lies side-by-side with his comrades-in-arms, North and South. The Union soldiers lie facing their Confederate adversaries. Linden Grove is one of only a few cemeteries in the nation which honors soldiers who fought on both sides of the conflict. Kentucky was a state where the phrase "brother against brother" rang true.

# About

## The

### Book

# Fact vs. Fiction: A Word from the Author

This is a work of fiction. As such, history becomes the setting on which plot and characters are developed. The purpose of this book is not intended to be an academic discussion of the Civil War, its battles, generals, causes, or ramifications. The purpose of this book, and any work of fiction, is primarily to entertain. If a reader learns something along the way, is led to further inquiry, or develops a new perspective, that is, of course, gratifying to the historical novelist. If a reader gains empathy for a time, a place, a people—that author has succeeded.

*Jesse: 53rd Kentucky* is inspired by the genealogical and military records of my Great-Grandfather Jesse J. Cook. It is inspired by the regimental records and battle stories from the mounted infantry units in Kentucky. Much of the color and events in the book are based on reporting from the local newspapers of the day, both in Covington, Kentucky, and Cincinnati, Ohio.

Uppermost in any novelist's mind is plot development. No one wants to read a story where nothing happens. To facilitate that end, my characters—whether soldiers or family members—are thrust into the action. Everything in the book is based on fact; however, Jesse's platoon, or the family, may not have been involved as described. There's just no way of knowing. That's the fictionalized part. The events all happened: the attacks on the railroads and passenger trains, the stand at the bridge in Marion, the raid through

Wytheville, the destruction of the lead mine, and the assault on the saltworks. The ride to Cumberland Gap took place with Jesse's company involved. The events in Covington are true. Unionists were celebrating in the most raucous of ways. Jesse's wounding, hospitalization, and the steamboat transport are based on fact, matching the dates stated in his pension files.

Jesse and the members of his family are factual, as described in "About Jesse." The members of Jesse's platoon are fictional, including Pete. They are intended to represent all soldiers of any company, in any regiment, of the Civil War. Jesse certainly would have experienced the camaraderie and the pain as depicted in the story. Hiram and Effie Gentry are also fictional, but Catherine Gentry did have family in the Virginia hills. I just hit a brick wall with the genealogical research. Some things are lost to history.

I grew up in the same town as Jesse. I walked the same streets, sat on the same riverbank, admired the same bridge, loved and dreamed at the same river. It was easy for me to write of that setting. And my great-grandfather? I felt his presence in inexplicable ways. He was with me during this writing process. I pray that the finished product does him justice, and I question how much I really invented.

Thanks for reading,
Ruth Webster

# The Bridge of Dreams

A modern view of the John A. Roebling Bridge
facing South, with Covington in background

The bridge in 1870, four years after completion
facing North, with Covington waterfront in foreground—streets
and structures that Jesse would have known well

(Both photos in Public Domain)

The iconic John A. Roebling Bridge has spanned the waters of the Ohio River between Covington and Cincinnati for over 150 years. It is a National Historic Landmark, still serving both pedestrian and vehicular traffic.

The first charter for the Covington-Cincinnati Bridge Company was granted by the Kentucky Legislature in 1846. (Kentucky owns the Ohio River—basically to the Ohio shoreline.) Due to intense opposition from ferryboat operators and steamboat companies, construction was delayed for ten years. There were also fears that a bridge would aid runaway slaves in reaching the North.

At the outbreak of the Civil War the towers on either side of the river were under construction. John Roebling had been hired early in the process to design the bridge. His son, Washington, was the engineer on site, who oversaw the construction and dealt with problems at hand. The project slowed during the first years of the war. Besides financial setbacks, both state legislatures had to approve lowering the required clearance of the bridge over the water. In 1863, work on the towers resumed, and continued through 1864. (This is when my character Pete Strong would have been employed on the crew.) Spinning of the cables began in November 1865 (meshing nicely with Jesse's discharge from the army in September when he's hoping to see construction of the bridge accelerate).

The newlywed Jesse and Eliza Cook, plus the rest of the family, were surely among the 166,000 people from Kentucky and Ohio who crossed the bridge on its opening weekend in early December 1866. They no doubt marveled at the then longest bridge in the world—later to be surpassed by Roebling's other bridge in Brooklyn.

Having grown up in Covington, I would hear of visitors saying, "Oh, doesn't this look like the Brooklyn Bridge." My reply, as a proud child of the Ohio River Valley, would inevitably be, "No, the Brooklyn Bridge looks like ours."

(Adapted from: A Quick History of the Roebling Suspension Bridge/ Covington-Cincinnati Suspension Bridge Committee)
http://www.roeblingbridge.org/history

# Who's Who:  Historical Figures

## <u>Union</u>

### Burbridge, Stephen G.

During the Civil War, Stephen Gano Burbridge was Kentucky's most controversial military commander. Born in Georgetown, Kentucky, on August 19, 1831, Burbridge practiced law and also owned a large plantation at the beginning of the war. In 1861, Burbridge was commissioned as colonel, and in June 1862, he was promoted to brigadier general. In 1864, after seeing combat at Shiloh, Vicksburg, and Port Gibson, Burbridge returned to Kentucky where he fought against Confederate raiders, particularly John Hunt Morgan. In August 1864, following his promotion to brevet major general, Burbridge was placed in command of the Department of Kentucky. His predecessor, Jermiah T. Boyle had alienated many loyal Kentuckians because of his harsh counterinsurgency tactics. Yet, Burbridge continued many of these policies, which included the arrest of Confederate sympathizers and suspected guerrillas. In addition, he ordered that four captured guerrillas be executed for each Union man killed by insurgents. Burbridge quickly lost the support of Kentuckians and was replaced in 1865. At the end of (that year), he resigned his commission and moved to Brooklyn, New York. He died there on November 30, 1894.

Aloma Williams Dew, "Stephen Gano Burbridge," in John E. Kleber, ed., The Kentucky Encyclopedia (Lexington: University of Kentucky, 1992), 142.

(From Stephen G. Burbridge/ The Filson Historical Society)
https://filsonhistorical.org/stephen-g-burbridge

## Gillem, Alan Cullem

Born in Gainesboro, Tennessee, General Gillem was a graduate of the West Point class of 1851. His first commission was in the field artillery branch of the army, serving in the Seminole Wars and in Texas.

At the outbreak of the Civil War, Gillem was promoted to captain and served as the Chief Quartermaster of the Army of the Ohio. During the Shiloh Campaign, then Major Gillem commanded the siege artillery. In 1862 he was named colonel of the Tenth Tennessee Infantry, then provost marshall of Nashville. He quickly rose to adjutant general of the State of Tennessee. Troops under his command killed General John Hunt Morgan in September 1864. Later that year he served under Major General George Stoneman at the Battle of Marion and Saltville.

Post-war, Gillem commanded the Fourth Military District under Reconstruction and participated and approved the new constitution being written for Arkansas's readmittance into the Union. His last command was in California against the Modoc Indians. He died in Tennessee in 1875.

## Hobson, Edward H.

General Edward Hobson was born in Greensburg, Kentucky—son of a steamboat captain and merchant, with whom he entered business. By the outbreak of the Civil War, the younger Hobson had served in the Mexican-American War and became director of a branch of the Bank of Kentucky.

Hobson organized the 13th Kentucky Infantry with the rank of colonel. He commanded his regiment with such success at Shiloh that he was promoted to brigadier general through the intervention of Abraham Lincoln. Placed in command of Union troops in Kentucky, he was ordered to watch the movements of Confederate General John Hunt Morgan. Hobson pursued Morgan during the latter's raid into Ohio in 1863, inflicting a serious defeat on that force—capturing Morgan and many of his cavalrymen. Later, Hobson was captured and released by none-other-than Morgan near Cynthiana, Kentucky. He commanded a brigade of Kentucky mounted infantry at the First Battle of Saltville (Author's note: not Stoneman's raid).

After the war, Hobson returned home to his business. He was involved in Republican politics but never managed to get himself elected to office. His support of Ulysses S. Grant for president garnered

Hobson the reward of being named District Collector of Internal Revenue. By 1887, he was president of the Southern Division of the Chesapeake and Ohio Railway.

A staunch supporter of the veterans' organization, the Grand Army of the Republic, Hobson died in Cleveland at a GAR encampment.

(Adapted from: Edward H. Hobson—Wikipedia)

## Stoneman, George Jr.

General George Stoneman was a native of New York State, a member of the West Point Class of 1846. Early in his military career Stoneman served in the Mormon Battalion, supporting the U.S. occupation of California. He became a proficient Indian fighter, served as quartermaster during the Mexican War, and eventually attained the rank of senior captain in the 5th U.S. Cavalry stationed in Texas.

When General George McClellan was promoted to command of the Army of the Potomac, Stoneman became Chief of Cavalry. The role of cavalry was little appreciated by McClellan, thus Stoneman and his troops were misused during the Peninsula Campaign in 1862. A later conflict with General Joseph Hooker resulted in Stoneman taking the blame for losses not of his making.

On a raid that Stoneman led to ostensibly free captives from the Andersonville Confederate prison camp, he himself was captured—the highest-ranking officer captured during the war.

In late 1864 Stoneman salvaged his reputation by conducting the raid that is the subject of this book. He would lead one more raid into North Carolina and Virginia in March 1865, nearly capturing Confederate President Jefferson Davis.

Stoneman retired in 1871 and moved to California, a locale for which he yearned. He served as Railroad Commissioner, and was later elected Governor of California, serving a four-year term beginning in 1882.

Stoneman was not nominated for a second term. One calamity followed another. He lost his ranch home to fire. He became estranged from his wife over her alleged affair. Broken financially and in poor health, he returned to New York where he died at his sister's home in Buffalo in 1894.

(Adapted from George Stoneman: Civil War General and California Governor.)
http://www.militarymuseum.org/Stoneman.html

# Who's Who: Historical Figures

## Confederacy

### Breckinridge, John C.

John C. Breckinridge of Kentucky was the youngest man ever to be elected Vice-President of the United States at the age of 35. He served alongside James Buchanan in the administration previous to that of Abraham Lincoln.

When war broke out Breckinridge chose to serve the Confederacy—immediately being branded a traitor. He was commissioned as a brigadier general and commanded a brigade at the Battle of Shiloh. Engagements under the command of General Braxton Bragg at Murfreesboro, Chickamauga, and Chattanooga kept Breckinridge involved in the western theater of the war. He had a contentious relationship with Bragg. Bragg would order Breckinridge to conduct questionable offensive military strategies and then blame him in the case of defeat. He also accused Breckinridge of drunkenness, a non-substantiated charge.

Breckinridge would collaborate successfully with General Jubal Early in raids near Washington before he was given a command of his own in Western Virginia. He was the victor at the First Battle of Saltville in 1864, but as supplies and manpower vanished (as related in this book) his later efforts at Saltville and Marion were futile.

In January, 1865, Breckinridge was appointed the final Confederate Secretary of War. He served ably, stressing an organized end to the war, convincing President Jefferson Davis not to prolong hostilities through guerrilla activity.

A hunted man, Breckinridge managed to escape to Cuba, then to the British Isles. He eventually reunited with his family in Canada. Pardoned in 1869, Breckinridge returned home to Lexington resuming his law practice. He refused repeatedly to reenter the political realm, choosing instead to serve as president of a Kentucky railroad and the Kentucky branch of an insurance company. He died in 1875 at the age of 54.

(Adapted from: John C. Breckinridge—Facts & Summary—HISTORY.com
https://www.history.com/topics/john-c-breckinridge )

## Duke, Basil W.

Basil Duke's most noted Civil War service was as second-in-command to his brother-in-law John Hunt Morgan. He rode with Morgan throughout the latter's infamous raids in Kentucky, Indiana, and Ohio. Duke's most lasting contribution to the war, however, was as an historian who chronicled the exploits of Morgan's Raiders and wrote tirelessly on behalf of the Southern cause. He was instrumental in establishing the Shiloh National Military Park and served as its commissioner at the behest of

Theodore Roosevelt. Duke was among the founders of the Filson Historical Society in Louisville.

A Kentucky native, he graduated from Transylvania University in Lexington and set up law practice in Missouri. He was in Missouri at the outbreak of the war and contributed to that state's futile efforts at secession. Eventually, he was indicted for treason but managed to escape to Kentucky. His first service in the Confederate military sent him back to Missouri, but by October of 1861 he had enlisted in Morgan's cavalry. Duke was the principal trainer for mounted combat with Morgan's Raiders. He purportedly loved fighting, was steadfast in battle, and "gently ordered" those under his command, which made him beloved.

Duke was captured at the Battle of Buffington Island in July 1863. He would remain in prison until his exchange one year later. In September of 1864, after Morgan was killed, Duke assumed command of the remnants of their forces. He was promoted to brigadier general and sent to Virginia (where he appears in this story).

After the Battles of Saltville and Marion, Duke would stand with the heart of the Confederacy. He was with Jefferson Davis shortly after that President fled Richmond. He attended the last war council of the Confederacy and surrendered in May 1865 in Georgia.

Twice wounded during the Civil War, Basil Duke would nonetheless live well into the Twentieth Century. His post-war life included stints as a commonwealth attorney in the State of Kentucky as well as chief counsel and lobbyist for the Louisville and Nashville Railroad. Ironically, the L&N was one of the main victims of Morgan's Raiders during the war.

(Adapted from: Basil W. Duke—Wikipedia
https://en.wikipedia.org/wiki/Basil_W._Duke )

## Giltner, Henry L.

Colonel Henry Giltner was from Carrollton, Kentucky, son of a farmer. In adulthood, Giltner owned the ferry at Carrollton and was elected sheriff of Carroll County for two terms previous to the Civil War. At the outbreak of war, he resigned his position as sheriff and entered the Confederate army as a private (despite the fact that he was educated at Hanover College in Indiana).

Giltner was sent to Virginia where he became the aid-de-camp to General Humphrey Marshall. By 1862 he returned to Kentucky to recruit a regiment for Marshall's brigade. The regiment would be known as the Fourth Kentucky Cavalry (the unit which opposed Jesse at the bridge in Marion). Giltner and his men served with Generals William E. Jackson and John S. Williams in East Tennessee. They were at the siege of Knoxville, fought in West Virginia and engagements at Mt. Sterling and Cynthiana in Kentucky. Giltner surrendered his forces at Mt. Sterling on April 30, 1865. Post-war, Giltner returned to Carrollton, making a living in farming and the marble business.

(Adapted from: The Biographical Encyclopaedia of Kentucky, published by J.M. Armstrong in 1878. Col. Henry L. Giltner

)

# Bibliography

"53rd Regiment Mounted Infantry." The Civil War Archive. Union Regimental Histories. Kentucky. 10 Oct. 2011. http://www.civilwararchive.com/Unreghst/unkyinf5.htm.

"Battle of Marion." Wikipedia, the free encyclopedia. 26 June 2014. 20 Jan. 2015. http://en.wikipedia.org/wiki/Battle_of_Marion.

"Battle Summary: Saltville, VA." CWSAC Battle Summaries. 20 Jan. 2015. http://www.cr.nps.gov/hps/abpp/battles/va082.htm.

"Christmas in the American Civil War." Wikipedia, the free encyclopedia. 10 Oct. 2017. https://en.wikipedia.org/wiki/Christmas_in_the_American_Civil_War .

"Cooper (profession)." Wikipedia, the free encyclopedia. 02 Feb. 2015. 16 Feb. 2015. http://en.wikipedia.org/wiki/Cooper_(profession).

"Crab Orchard, Kentucky." Wikipedia, the free encyclopedia. 22 Jan. 2015. http://en.wikipedia.org/Crab_Orchard,_Kentucky.

"Historical Perspective on the American Economy, A." *American History: From Revolution to Reconstruction and Beyond*. University of Groningen – Humanities Computing, 1994-2012 GMW. 16 Feb. 2015. http://www.let.rug.nl/usa/outlines/economy-1991/a-historical-perspective-on-the-american .

"History of the 42-Gallon Oil Barrel." American Oil & Gas Historical Society. 16 Feb. 2015. http://aoghs.org/transportation/history-of-the-42-gallon-oil-barrel/.

"Kentucky in the American Civil War." Wikipedia, the free encyclopedia. 19 Feb. 2018. https://en.wikipedia.org/wiki/Kentucky_in_the_American_Civil_War .

"Louisville and Nashville Railroad." Wikipedia, the free encyclopedia. 22 Jan. 2015. http://en.wikipedia.org/wiki/Louisville_and_Nashville_Railroad#19th_century.

"Saltville Battlefields Historic District." 12 Oct. 2014. 20 Jan. 2015. http://en.wikipedia.org/wiki/Saltville_Battlefields_Historic_District.

"Saltville's Historic Civil War Battles." Museum of the Middle Appalachians. 20 Jan. 2015. http://www.museum-mid-app.org/civil-war.htm.

"Second Battle of Saltville." CivilWarWiki. 15 May 2013. 20 Jan. 2015. http://civilwarwiki.net/wiki/Second_Battle_of_Saltville.

Dietzen, Lizzie. "Saltville During the Civil War." Encyclopedia Virginia. 6 Feb. 2012. 20 Jan. 2015. http://www.encyclopediavirginia.org/Saltville_During_the_Civil_War

Foote, Shelby. *The Civil War, A Narrative: Red River to Appomattox*. New York: Vantage Books, a Division of Random House, 1974.

Gorman, Kathleen L. "Civil War Pensions." Essential Civil War Curriculum. 18 Feb. 2018. http://www.essentialcivilwarcurriculum.com/civil-war-pensions.html.

Gragg, Rod. *From Fields of Fire and Glory: Letters of the Civil War*. San Francisco: Chronicle Books, 2002.

Wimberg, Robert J. *Cincinnati and the Civil War: 1864*. Cincinnati: Ohio Book Store, Publishers, 2014.

Wimberg, Robert J. *Cincinnati and the Civil War: 1865*. Cincinnati: Ohio Book Store, Publishers, 2015.

Newspapers.com—the digitized repository of historic newspapers.

# About the Series

## Toe the Mark

(Based on the lives and military records of actual soldiers.)

Book One—*Henry: The Jersey Brigade*

Henry Marts is a seaman—oysterman—living in South Jersey at the outbreak of the Civil War. He has to justify fighting for the Union, for Henry is a devout Quaker. His family is torn on how best to show resistance to the troubles dividing the nation. Henry will enlist in the newly formed Jersey Third Regiment, one of the first volunteer regiments in the entire nation. His service will last for three years, through some of the fiercest fighting in Virginia, until the day he climbs Laurel Hill at Spotsylvania Courthouse.

Book Two—*Jesse: 53rd Kentucky*

Book Three—*Cousins at War (coming 2019)*

Two pairs of brothers. Two sets of cousins. Two opposing sides. One war. Francis Marion Allender, one of Morgan's Raiders, will face his first cousin Sam Stallcup and the Sixth Ohio at Murfreesboro. Marion's brother Alex and cousin Francis Marion Stallcup will both ride for the Union. In Kentucky, a state divided, family ties rupture, as each man's beliefs are sorely tested.

Book Four—*Title TBA*

Charles W. Webster is a civilian, the States Attorney for Frederick County in the State of Maryland. Outspoken, well-respected, and a staunch Unionist, Webster will find himself a target in Confederate General

J.E.B. Stuart's raid through Maryland on the road to Gettysburg.

Book Five—*Title TBA*

Benjamin Franklin Ramsey was an orphan, raised by an elder sister, trained as a shoemaker by her husband. But Ben's interest in that trade will wane with the Civil War. Initially enlisting in the Ohio Boat Service, Ben serves on a gunboat on America's interior rivers. But it is the artillery on that boat which captures his imagination. Ben's second enlistment will be with the 21st Ohio Battery, where he rides under General Stoneman on that most infamous raid into the South.

Book Six—*Title TBA*

It is 1876, the Centennial of the United States of America. The great War of Rebellion (or Civil War) has been over for ten years. The young men of that war are in the prime of their lives—Marts, Cook, Stallcup, and Ramsey. Many veterans from the Union Army have proudly joined the ranks of the Grand Army of the Republic. They will descend upon Philadelphia, site of the Centennial Exhibition, to celebrate and recollect as America enters its second century.

# About the Author

Ruth Ann Ochs Webster was born and raised in Covington, Kentucky, a not quite Northern and not quite Southern town on the Ohio River. That location sparked a lifelong interest in both history and travel. Ruth now lives in metro Pittsburgh, near the confluence of the two rivers that form the Ohio. She is a retired National Board-Certified Teacher, having specialized in language arts and United States History.

Ruth has been published in magazines, literary journals, and newspapers. She was a newspaper columnist for seven years. She is the recipient of the Backbone Mountain Review Fiction Prize, the Stanier Award from the Pittsburgh International Children's Festival (a collaboration), and the 2017 Author Zone (TAZ) Award for Historical Fiction—1st Place, for *Henry: The Jersey Brigade*.

Website: www.ruthochswebster.com
Social Media: Facebook.com/ruthochswebsterauthor